'**Sometimes you think what, *ma princesse*?**' he whispered.

'Don't, Pierre! Don't call me by that name. You know how—'

She broke off as she felt her treacherous body reacting to his closeness.

His lips claimed hers and she gave in, lovingly, to his gentle kiss. But a gentle kiss was not enough. Her body needed consummation.

'No!' She moved suddenly as the feelings of wild abandonment threatened to engulf her senses. She wanted Pierre so much, but she mustn't allow herself to get carried away. 'Oh, Pierre,' she said softly. 'What are we going to do?'

'You're the one who changed the rules, Alyssa. Are you telling me that you still have feelings for me in spite of—?'

'If only you knew!' she said, her body aching with the frustration and futility of the situation. 'If only—'

She broke off. She'd said too much already.

As a full-time writer, mother and grandmother, **Margaret Barker** says: 'I feel blessed with my lifestyle, which has evolved over the years and included working as a State Registered Nurse. My husband and I live in a sixteenth-century thatched house near the East Anglian Coast. We are still very much in love, which helps when I am describing the romantic feelings of my heroines. In fact, if I find the creative flow diminishing, my husband will often suggest we put in some more research into the romantic aspects that are eluding me at the time!'

Recent titles by the same author:

THE SPANISH DOCTOR
THE GREEK SURGEON
A CHRISTMAS TO REMEMBER
THE PREGNANT DOCTOR

CHRISTMAS IN PARIS

BY
MARGARET BARKER

MILLS & BOON®

First published in Great Britain 2002
Harlequin Mills & Boon Limited,
Eton House, 18-24 Paradise Road, Richmond, Surrey TW9 1SR

© Margaret Barker 2002

ISBN 0 263 83111 6

Set in Times Roman 10½ on 12 pt.
03-1202-50056

Printed and bound in Spain
by Litografia Rosés, S.A., Barcelona

CHAPTER ONE

ALYSSA paused at the foot of the wide, sweeping steps that led to the revolving glass door. *Une grande porte à tambour,* Pierre had called it. She was relieved to find that her French was coming back, although she'd found the conversation with the taxi driver coming across Paris from the Gare du Nord station had been a bit of a strain. She could understand Parisians who spoke like her mother, but the taxi driver had had a strong accent from the south of France, and he'd chatted so quickly it had been difficult to follow him.

Alyssa hadn't spoken much French in the eight years since she'd worked in this very building with Pierre. The knot in her stomach tightened as she thought about him, his wonderful eyes when he'd turned to look down at her, the touch of his tantalising fingers on her skin...

She shivered, as if someone had walked over her grave. Maybe she shouldn't have come back here. Perhaps it was all going to be too poignant, walking along the white corridors of the Clinique Ste Catherine when Pierre was no longer there.

A young, tall, fair-haired man was hurrying along the road towards the *clinique*. He stopped and smiled at Alyssa, pointing to her suitcase, which she'd dumped on the pavement whilst she indulged herself in poignant memories of that other time, now so long ago.

'Puis-je vous aider, mademoiselle?'

Alyssa smiled at the helpful young man, replying in French that it was kind of him to offer to help her, but she

5

could manage to carry her suitcase up the steps to the *clinique*.

The young man smiled back, giving a Gallic shrug which seemed to imply that he wasn't going to allow a small, slightly built blonde to carry a heavy suitcase up the steps when he was going that way. Bending down, he heaved up the suitcase as if it were an empty plastic bag.

Frenchmen are so gallant! Alyssa thought as she walked beside him, relieved that she didn't have to carry that heavy suitcase any more. It had been bad enough getting it from the Eurostar into a taxi and from the taxi to the foot of the steps.

The young man introduced himself as Dr Jacques Suchet. *'Et vous êtes…?'*

'I'm Alyssa Ferguson.'

'Ah, our new English doctor. Welcome to the Clinique Ste Catherine. I thought maybe that was who you were, but your French is so good you could almost pass for a Parisian.'

Alyssa smiled. 'You're very kind. My mother was born in Paris and I used to speak fluently with her as a child, but I've spoken only English for the past eight years,' she said as she negotiated the revolving doors behind Dr Suchet.

He looked very young to be a doctor and couldn't have been qualified very long. He had that devil-may-care, zest-for-life attitude that had typified Pierre when she'd first met him. She'd followed Pierre in through these very doors so often. Sometimes he'd turned to give her a clandestine kiss, laughing at her prim concern when she'd glanced over to look at the staff on the reception desk.

She'd been so young then, only twenty-one, and Pierre had been twenty-nine. Her own age now, so Pierre must be thirty-seven. She reckoned he would still be handsome, and probably tanned from all that sun out there in the West Indies. He'd used to have a permanent suntan here in Paris from jogging every day in the Bois de Boulogne, she remembered fondly, and he'd looked so fantastic in that dark blue tracksuit she'd helped him choose in the sports shop on the Rue de Passy.

She swallowed hard. Yes, it had been a mistake to come back here, but she had to make the best of it now.

Whatever had possessed her to answer that advertisement in that medical magazine? Nostalgia was a terrible affliction! But she'd felt drawn to come back. It was as if a magnetic force was dragging her away from London to make this journey to Paris. Deep down she was hoping that she would be able to lay the ghost to rest. Get rid of her constant yearning for those idyllic days of her affair with Pierre.

'I expect you'll have to report to our medical director.'

Dr Suchet put her suitcase down on the tiled floor in the reception area, looking down at Alyssa enquiringly. 'What exactly are your instructions, Dr Ferguson?'

'Oh, please, call me Alyssa.'

'What a beautiful name! And you must call me Jacques.'

Alyssa hesitated. 'Jacques, I was told to come to the *clinique* and...'

Her voice trailed away and her legs seemed to turn to jelly. She put out her hand to place her fingers on Dr Suchet's arm, in case she fainted with the shock. The tall, dark man coming towards her looked unmistakably like Pierre. But he couldn't be Pierre! Pierre wasn't here. Pierre lived and worked in the West Indies. There wasn't the remotest chance that this was happening. It was a dream. She must have fainted and dreamed that...

'Hello, Alyssa.'

The dream was holding out his hand. And there was no

mistaking the voice. She would know that voice anywhere, and the handshake—firm, deeply disturbing. Frissons of excitement tinged with apprehension ran through her.

'Pierre, why are you here?' Her faint voice sounded strange even to her own ears.

His dark eyes held her gaze. 'I could ask you the same question, Alyssa. What made you come back?'

Dr Suchet gave a discreet cough. 'I believe that introductions do not seem to be necessary, so I will leave the two of you together. Obviously, Dr Alyssa Ferguson, you have previously met our *médecin-chef*—the medical director of the *clinique*—Dr Pierre Dupont.'

Alyssa stared at Pierre, her heart beating rapidly. Had she heard Jacques correctly? Was Pierre really the medical director of the *clinique* now?

'But I was interviewed by Dr Cheveny. He told me he would be here as director when…'

'Dr Cheveny had a heart attack last week. I happened to be in Paris on a three-month holiday. François Cheveny is an old friend of mine and he asked me to take over the *clinique* temporarily until he has recovered.'

Pierre glanced around the reception area, where work seemed to have stopped. All eyes of the clerical and nursing staff were on the couple in the centre of the tiled floor.

'Come into my consulting room,' Pierre said quietly. 'We can't talk here.'

He bent down and picked up her suitcase.

As she followed Pierre down the white corridor her head was spinning at the completely unexpected turn of events. Pierre looked exactly the same. Still handsome—slightly older, perhaps. In the brief moment when their eyes had met she'd noticed a tired expression which hadn't been there when she'd first known him. But his dark hair was still thick and luxuriantly shining, with a couple of strands falling over his face, though she'd detected the beginnings of lines on his forehead and at the sides of his eyes.

As she walked through the door of his consulting room she was still in a state of shock. But beyond the feeling of shock she was deeply aware of the turbulence of her emotions. When she'd written that letter to Pierre, eight years ago, she'd planned never to see him again. It was madness to meet up like this! And if Pierre was medical director here she would have to come into contact with him every day. And he would ask her why...

'Do sit down, Alyssa.'

Pierre was holding the back of a deep, buttoned leather armchair. She sat down, rigidly at first, and then more relaxed as Pierre released his grip on her chair and moved over to the other side of the large, beautifully polished mahogany desk. For a moment she allowed her eyes to roam around her surroundings, admiring the book-lined walls, the deep pile of the luxurious carpet. She'd forgotten just how luxurious the Clinique Ste Catherine was. A great deal different from the hospital where she'd been working in London.

'So, how are you, Alyssa?' Pierre's voice was cool and impersonal as he faced her across the desk.

'I'm fine. How are you, Pierre?'

This was ridiculous! Two ex-lovers conducting an excruciatingly embarrassing conversation. Alyssa longed to get up from her chair, kick off her shoes, run round the desk and put her arms around Pierre. He was looking as uncomfortable as she felt.

'I'm in good health,' Pierre replied. 'A little disconcerted by the fact that you're here. It was only this morning that I checked through the latest staffing arrangements and saw that you were coming to join us. I must admit it was the last thing I expected.'

'I didn't know you would be here, Pierre,' Alyssa said quietly.

'Well, obviously!' Pierre's brown eyes flashed.

He leaned back in his chair, placing the points of his long, slender, tapering fingers together in front of him. It was an endearing gesture that Alyssa remembered so well. It meant he was giving the problem his undivided attention. She leaned forward to explain, but Pierre continued after the pause.

'You made it quite clear in your last letter that you never wanted to see me again.'

'I'm sure I wasn't as brusque as that.'

Pierre waved a hand in the air, as if to dismiss her argument. 'You were utterly explicit that you wanted to end our affair. You said that you found it difficult to continue to commit to a serious relationship whilst you were studying to be a doctor. And you said that when you were qualified your career would come first.'

Alyssa winced inwardly. Had she really been so brutal to the man she still loved with all her heart? But, because she loved him, she hadn't been able to tell him the real reason. That really would have broken his heart. No, she'd had no choice. She'd had to call a halt, sooner rather than later, so the white lies had been inevitable.

'I was finding it hard to concentrate on my work when…'

'Are you sure that was the real reason?' he said, with steely calm. 'Obviously our relationship meant nothing to you. I found it hard to believe that you could cool down so quickly.'

If he'd only known the agony she'd been going through at the time! Yes, she would have loved to put her head on his shoulder, to sob her heart out and have him commiserate with her misfortune, but that would have only prolonged the time before their inevitable split.

She took a deep breath. 'Pierre, I don't think I'll be able to work here at the *clinique* now that I know you're the medical director. I realise that it would be difficult for you to have me working on your staff, so…'

'Oh, please don't give up so easily! You're committed to a contract, remember? Or is any kind of commitment onerous for you?'

Looking across the desk at the hard expression on Pierre's face, she felt as if a knife was being driven through her heart. She leaned back in her chair and closed her eyes for a moment, to blot out the sight of the man she still loved. It was her love for him that prevented her from explaining the truth to him.

A deep weariness was stealing over her. The train journey through the channel tunnel had been slow, due to a temporary breakdown, and it was hours since she'd left London this morning. She couldn't take much more of this cross-questioning that would lead nowhere. Nor could she bear to work with the man she loved under these hostile conditions. Unbidden, a tear escaped from underneath her tightly shut eyelids. Her head felt light—as if it was full of cotton wool.

'Alyssa, are you all right?'

She felt Pierre's hand on her shoulder and opened her eyes, aware that they were moist and displaying far too much emotion. Looking up, she saw deep concern etched on Pierre's strikingly handsome face. For a brief, mad moment she expected him to bend down and kiss the tears away from her cheek. But that was yesterday—long, long ago. This was today, when her life had changed so much.

'Yes, yes, I'm OK,' she said quickly.

Pierre reached for a tissue from the box on his desk and, leaning forward, dabbed her eyes with his gentle touch.

'I don't know why you're crying,' he said, his voice oh, so soft, just as she remembered it used to be. 'Do I have such a terrible effect on you that you can't bear to be near me?'

She raised her hand and caught hold of his wrist. His tender expression changed to one of surprise and he stood stock still, looking down at her.

She cleared her throat. If only she could tell him the truth! No, she mustn't! She let go of his wrist, clasping her hands in front of her so that she wouldn't be tempted to make physical contact again.

'I'm just tired, that's all,' she said quickly. 'Travelling always has this effect on me. I remember coming over on the boat train to France with my mother as a child. I was always exhausted when we arrived at the Gare du Nord, and my mother would put me straight to bed when we reached Grand-maman's apartment.'

Pierre leaned back against the desk, his expression more relaxed and open. 'How is your mother, Alyssa? I never met her, but you told me so much about her when you were here in Paris before that I feel I know her.'

'Maman…' Alyssa faltered, as she always did when she thought about her mother. 'Unfortunately, she developed an incurable cancer. She died some years ago.'

'I'm so sorry.'

Alyssa swallowed hard. 'I would have liked you to meet her.'

Now, that was the sort of remark she mustn't make if she was going to see this contract through! It must be strictly professional from now on.

'Yes, it was a pity I didn't meet her when we…when

you were in Paris before,' Pierre said quietly. 'Now, let's get down to business.'

He returned to the other side of the desk. 'I'd like to suggest that we don't refer to…to what happened between us again. You obviously had your reasons for terminating our affair and I will respect that. Simply do your job as efficiently as you can. Dr Cheveny hopes to be back here after Christmas. That's when I have to return to the West Indies. It's now November, so we only have to work together for a few weeks. Do you think you can manage that?'

Alyssa nodded. 'Of course. I'm looking forward to working here as a doctor. Eight years ago—as temporary medical assistant and general dogsbody, at the end of my third year of medical school—some of the work I had to do was pretty boring and repetitive, but now…!'

She smiled, feeling herself relax again. Yes, it would work. She would *make* it work.

Pierre smiled, and Alyssa could see some of his erst-while boyish charm returning. 'You were a very pretty general dogsbody, if I may say so.'

Alyssa wanted to tell Pierre that he mustn't make remarks like that if their professional relationship was going to work. But, looking at the glorious smile on his beauti-fully shaped mouth as she watched him across the desk, she tried to tell herself she could handle the occasional compliment from him. She'd been starved of this sort of warm feeling for far too long.

'I understand I qualify for a room in the medics' quarters now,' Alyssa said quickly.

Pierre nodded. 'I'll ask the housekeeper to show you up there.' He picked up the phone and gave the necessary instructions. 'You don't start work until tomorrow, so you'll have time to settle in.'

Now he was standing up, very much the efficient medical director who wanted to terminate this interview and get on with his important job.

The housekeeper arrived to escort her to the medical staff quarters. Alyssa gave a backward glance as she left Pierre's room, but he was already immersed in his paperwork, giving the impression that she was just another employee who'd taken up his time.

As he listened to the sound of Alyssa's small feet retreating down the corridor Pierre closed his eyes and leaned heavily against the back of his chair. The shock of seeing Alyssa again had been emotionally shredding. Eight years ago, when he'd received that heartbreaking letter, he'd been unable to comprehend how Alyssa could do such a thing. He'd adored her, worshipped her, known without a shadow of a doubt that she was the only woman he could ever love.

And then, out of the blue, her letter had arrived, tearing his heart into pieces and turning him into a nervous wreck for weeks on end. He'd thought of phoning to see if Alyssa was ill, or had taken leave of her senses, but then he'd reprimanded himself severely. The plain fact of the matter was that he'd obviously misjudged Alyssa's character. They'd only known each other for three months, after all. She must have been putting on an act for him until it was time for her to return to England.

For eight years he'd tried to be sensible about the situation. He'd told himself to get on with his life and forget Alyssa. But he couldn't forget her. She'd been his whole world for three months and he'd planned to spend the rest of his life with her. Whenever he'd tried to enjoy a brief relationship with someone he'd found himself comparing them with Alyssa, the love of his life, and had given up on the idea of continuing.

So how was he going to handle this situation? He could simply have agreed with Alyssa when she'd said they couldn't work together and that she ought to leave. That would have been the sensible course of action. But, having met her again, he couldn't bear to have her disappear once more. That was why he'd reacted so sharply—worried that she might simply stand up and walk out through the door.

He would try not to become emotionally involved, because obviously Alyssa was the sort of girl who didn't want a serious relationship. Just having her near him until his temporary directorship of the *clinique* ended after Christmas would be enough...wouldn't it?

He would have to play it cool, as he hoped he'd done just now. Alyssa mustn't have any idea how he longed to reach out and take her in his arms, to feel that soft silky skin against his hardening body. Perhaps if Alyssa thought he'd got over their affair she might agree to come out with him one evening on a light-hearted date—something like a trip to the theatre with supper in a restaurant afterwards, perhaps a trip in a *bateau mouche* on the River Seine one evening, with dinner in the floating restaurant, looking out at the twinkling lights of Paris on either side of the river.

Nothing too romantic, of course! He would be happy just to be with Alyssa. But she mustn't know how deeply he felt about her or that would send her running away again.

Pierre's internal phone was ringing. He picked it up and listened to the voice of his secretary.

'Excuse me, sir, the doctors for the medical conference you asked for will be assembled in the lecture hall this evening. They would like to know how long you will require them to be in conference with you.'

Pierre glanced down at the notes he'd prepared for his inaugural talk with the senior medical staff of the clinic. 'About an hour, Sidonie.'

He put down the phone, rose from his desk and went over to the window. Henri, the middle-aged gardener, was getting ready to cut the tall hedge at the end of the garden. Pierre remembered him from the time he'd last worked here. Dr Cheveny had told him that Henri had lovingly taken care of the large *clinique* garden since he took over from his father when he'd retired twenty years ago. Earlier on Pierre had seen Henri carefully tending the rose beds which were always so impressive during the summer months. Even now, in November, there were still a few blossoms among the green leaves.

The sight of the roses in the beautiful garden always revived Pierre's spirits. They reminded him of the lovely garden that surrounded his home on the island of Ste Cécile in the West Indies. He closed his eyes so that he could visualise it again. He could almost hear the enchanting sounds of the tropical birds who came every morning to be fed outside the kitchen door. Oh, he had such a wonderful home on his beautiful island! The only thing it lacked was the woman he loved—the woman he'd asked to be his wife.

Soon after he'd met Alyssa for the first time he'd known. That feeling of completeness, of oneness with another soul, could only come once in a lifetime. He was sure of that. And, foolishly, he'd thought he knew that Alyssa felt the same way, so he'd gone ahead and made his dreams into concrete plans.

He'd planned to marry Alyssa here in Paris, then take her out to the West Indies and start the family he longed for. Eight years on, his garden would by now be resounding with the noise of their children playing under the tall palm trees. Alyssa herself would perhaps be sitting in the shade of the veranda, feeding the latest baby. Alyssa knew he loved babies.

They'd discussed it just before she'd gone back to England, he remembered, on the night he'd asked her to marry him. She'd said she loved babies too, but wanted to finish her medical training before she thought about marriage. She'd wanted them to keep in contact with each other, and she'd given him absolutely no inkling of the fact that she had decided to call a halt to their relationship. At that point in time he'd had no idea that she was determined to remain independent for the rest of her life.

He turned away from the window, pressing his hands against the sides of his head, knowing that he mustn't dwell on what might have been. He would never put himself through the misery of having his heart broken again, so his emotions must remain on ice for the whole time Alyssa was working here at the *clinique*. He would enjoy an evening out with her if she agreed, just for old times' sake, but that was as far as it must go.

Alyssa's room at the back of the *clinique* faced west, so that now, looking through the open casement window, she could see the sun slanting down over the Bois de Boulogne. She was lucky to have a view of the immaculately maintained garden. This must be one of the most expensive gardens in Paris, because land and property prices in the sixteenth arrondissement didn't come cheap. The *clinique* could sell this land to a property developer and get a huge sum. But it was a well-established garden, and the *clinique* considered it essential that their patients should enjoy beautiful surroundings. It was all part of the healing process.

Although it was already the middle of November, there

were still roses in the garden, and splendid, carefully tended perennial shrubs. Out there, at the end of the garden, the gardener was standing on a ladder cutting a high hedge. Screwing up her eyes, she could see that it was the same friendly man who'd looked after the garden when she was first here. What was his name? Henri? Yes, that was it. She'd chatted to him sometimes when she'd sat on that seat over there and luxuriated in the summer sunshine.

The rasping hum of Henri's electric saw was disturbing the peace of the late afternoon, but the garden was an idyllic sight and she didn't mind the noise. It blended in with the general hum of Paris which was always there in the background, just like she remembered it had been when, as a child, she'd used to visit her grandmother in the nearby Rue de la Pompe. She would lie in her little bed, with its curved mahogany ends which had reminded her of a boat, listening to the continual, fascinating sounds of this great city, longing to be grown up so that she could go out at night and become a part of the excitement that she knew was always out there.

Her mother had always looked so glamorous when she dressed up and went out to the theatre. There had never been any lack of men-friends from her mother's former time in Paris, more than willing to escort a beautiful young widow to the theatre or a concert. And when her mother had gone Alyssa would sneak out of her room and go into the salon, where her grandmother would be working on her needlework.

She would tell her grandmother she couldn't sleep and Grand-maman would put down the needlework and open her arms towards her. Alyssa would run over to the sofa and snuggle up, knowing that she wouldn't have to go back to bed until she'd had a hot chocolate drink and maybe another of those *petit beurre* biscuits...

She sighed and sank down on to the bed. It was no good indulging in nostalgia all the time. Just look where it had got her! She lay back against the pillows as she cast her eyes around the room that was to be her home whilst she worked here at the *clinique*.

It had its own little shower room, complete with bidet and loo. Very French! The white cotton bedroom curtains were lined with a heavier linen mix material and looped back against the walls with ties; the shelves on the walls looked sadly empty as they waited to be filled with the few books Alyssa had been able to carry with her. She would have the joy of buying some more French books now she was in Paris again. But the afternoon sun, streaming through the windows, made up for the stark uniformity of this anonymous, functional room.

The last time she'd worked here at the clinic she hadn't qualified for a residential room. She'd been obliged to find her own cheap room on the ground floor of a nearby prestigious apartment block in the Rue de l'Assomption. In reality, it had been a *chambre de bonne*, a maid's room, which the owner, who didn't have a live-in maid, had decided to rent out. There had been a shower and loo down the corridor, she remembered, but she'd hated having to leave the safety of her room to visit those shared conveniences after dark.

But the deprivations of her living accommodation hadn't dispelled the euphoric feeling of happiness that had constantly enveloped her during the wonderful three months of her affair with Pierre. She'd never taken Pierre back to her room. The concierge would have fixed her with his beady eye as she'd walked past his little office. Visitors to the maids' quarters were actively discouraged. But she'd spent many nights at Pierre's apartment further down the road.

Pierre's apartment was where their baby had been conceived. That poor little mite who'd never stood a chance because he'd never got further than her left Fallopian tube. If only he could have found his way down into her womb she would have been able to nourish and cosset him and bring him to full term, and then...

She swallowed hard. She didn't like to dwell on the memory of that ill-fated ectopic pregnancy: the pain, the horror of knowing that she'd lost Pierre's baby—the baby she hadn't known was developing in her Fallopian tube when she'd said goodbye to Pierre at the Gare du Nord on that sunny September afternoon, her heart so full of love and longing to return to him as soon as possible.

She was only glad that Pierre had never known she'd been pregnant when she'd left him here in Paris. Pierre, who couldn't wait to be a father, who'd told her that he longed for a large family. Pierre, who'd begged her to marry him, to leave medical school and go with him to the West Indies so that they could start their wonderful family and live happily ever after.

But the dream had been well and truly shattered when her left Fallopian tube had been excised, with the unviable embryo inside it, and she'd been left with only one Fallopian tube together with some abdominal scarring and internal adhesions. Her gynaecologist had told her that it was unlikely she would be able to conceive again. So, loving Pierre as she did, knowing how much he wanted children, she'd taken the decision to put an end to their relationship.

It had been necessary to be cruel to be kind. At least by giving him his freedom from a relationship with her she was making sure that he could find someone who could have the babies he wanted.

She gave herself an inward shake and made a determined effort to climb off the bed. It was no good lying here expecting her case to unpack itself!

She suddenly realised that it was all quiet in the garden. The gardener must have finished his hedge and packed up for the day. She looked out of the window and as her eyes focused on the hedge she gave an involuntary gasp of dismay.

Henri had indeed finished working, but he was lying at the bottom of the hedge beside his fallen ladder and from where she was standing it looked as if he'd sustained a seriously damaging fall. He was completely silent and motionless.

Alyssa picked up the phone. Pierre's internal number was the only one she'd written on her notepad since arriving here. She dialled. *Please be there, otherwise…*

'Allo? Oui…'

Pierre's comforting voice helped to calm her. Yes, he would go out into the garden at once… Yes, her help would be invaluable…

Seconds later she was bending over Henri's motionless form while Pierre, who had already alerted extra staff, was making a clinical assessment from the other side.

A porter with a trolley came hurrying up the path.

'We need to put Henri on an orthopaedic slab before we take him inside on the trolley,' Pierre said quickly. 'There could be some damage to his neck. He had the ladder fully extended and he's fallen in an awkward position.'

The porter hurried back inside to return with a rigid plastic slab, specifically designed for trauma patients who might have suffered neck injuries. Carefully, Pierre and Alyssa eased their patient on to the slab, strapping him down so that Henri would sustain no further damage to his spine or limbs. With the help of the porter, they lifted him on to the trolley. As they did so, Henri opened his eyes.

Trying to move his head, their patient was irritated to find he was restrained by the head brace.

'Lie still, Henri,' Pierre said gently.

'What's happened?' Henri asked in a croaky voice.

'You've fallen from your ladder,' Alyssa said, taking hold of the frightened man's hand. 'We're going to take you inside the *clinique*.'

'My leg hurts.'

Alyssa held her patient's hand as they moved off down the garden path towards the door that led into the *clinique*. 'We're going to take care of you, Henri.'

'Have we met before?' Henri said, screwing up his eyes as he looked at Alyssa. 'Aren't you that little English girl who used to bring me coffee in the garden?'

Alyssa smiled. 'That's me. I've come back to work here.'

Henri momentarily winced with pain, but tried to carry on with his conversation. 'You haven't grown much, have you? You're still *très petite*.'

'Alyssa's a doctor now,' Pierre said, glad that the conversation was helping to keep Henri's mind off his unpleasant situation.

'She doesn't look like a doctor,' Henri said, in his brusque yet jocular manner. 'Anyway, it's nice to see you again, Alyssa. *Mon dieu!* Don't they have any painkillers in this—?'

'Coming up,' Pierre said as he reached for the syringe he'd prepared.

Looking down at Henri, Alyssa could see that he was a tough man. But the pain he was feeling now in his right leg was reducing him to tears. It was obvious from the unnatural angle of the leg that there was a multiple fracture around the area of the ankle.

She'd already removed Henri's shoe because his foot

was rapidly swelling. As soon as they got him inside they could make a real assessment of the damage.

Pierre helped the porter to manoeuvre the trolley into one of the treatment rooms and Alyssa found a pair of scissors and cut up the sides of Henri's trousers to expose the damaged limb.

Pierre's face was grave as he looked down at the splintered tibia bone which had pierced through the skin.

'Fractured tibia made worse by the fact that the talus bone appears to have been pushed up into it,' he said quietly to Alyssa. 'We'll get an X-ray.'

'Is my leg broken?' Henri asked.

'I'm afraid so,' Pierre said. 'We're going to have you X-rayed so that we'll know exactly how to treat it. I'm just going to give you an injection that will help with the pain.'

'Thanks, Pierre—I mean Dr Dupont. I heard that you'd taken over since Dr Cheveny's heart attack, so you're very important now.'

Pierre smiled. 'I'm just Pierre to old friends.'

Henri groaned with pain again. 'More painkillers, *s'il vous plaît*. My leg feels awful.'

'It looks as if you took the full weight of your fall on that one leg, Henri.' Pierre said, as he and Alyssa accompanied Henri into the X-ray department. 'I can't find any other area that's affected.'

'In that case can I come out of this neck brace? *Mon dieu!* It hurts like hell!'

'Not until we've had your neck X-rayed and you've been seen by a neurologist,' Alyssa said. 'You were out cold for a few minutes, and after a fall like you've sustained we've got to be sure your spine is uninjured.'

The radiographer took over for a while, to get the relevant X-rays.

As they waited in the ante-room, Pierre looked across at Alyssa. 'I read in your CV that you've had extensive experience in orthopaedics.'

'Yes, I toyed with the idea of specialising,' Alyssa said evenly.

Alone with Pierre again, even with the busy hospital staff in the next room, she was beginning to feel the strain of pretending that they'd never meant anything to each other.

'So why didn't you?' Pierre asked quietly.

'I was also very interested in obstetrics and gynaecology, so I would have had to make a difficult choice. And at the same time…' She hesitated. 'I felt I needed a change from my life in London. I needed to get away,' she said slowly, careful not to blurt out too much.

'So you thought you'd give Paris one more try, did you?' Pierre said lightly. 'Do the lights of Paris shine brighter than London?'

'Sometimes,' Alyssa said, remembering that she was supposed to be an independent, fun-loving woman whose interests revolved around theatre, entertainment, restaurants and enjoying herself.

It would be difficult to keep up this charade, but Pierre must never know how she longed for a home and babies. On her next birthday she would be thirty, and she could almost feel her biological clock ticking away inside. Thirty wasn't old, but it was time to take stock of her life. The emptiness of her constant social round in London was beginning to get to her, and Paris still had a warmth about it—mainly because she'd once been happier here than she'd ever been in her whole life, either before her relationship with Pierre or afterwards.

The radiographer, a tall, slim woman of about forty, came into the room with Henri's X-rays and switched on the screen which displayed them. Pierre and Alyssa went carefully through each one.

'You can see here where the foot took the full impact, forcing the talus up into the tibia, causing it to shatter into all these pieces we see floating around,' Pierre said, pointing to the injured lower leg.

Alyssa nodded. 'So, we've got massive problems with the ankle.'

'Our orthopaedic consultant is on his way over from another hospital. As you know, we have a number of consultants who work both here and at other hospitals in Paris. Yves Grandet is one of our top specialists. I've alerted the theatre staff about the possibility of an orthopaedic operation this evening, but we'll wait to see what Yves thinks when he arrives. He should be here any—'

Pierre broke off and smiled as a small man of about fifty in a dark grey pinstripe suit came into the room.

'Yves!' Pierre shook the newcomer by the hand. 'Thank you for coming so promptly. This is Dr Alyssa Ferguson, who has joined the staff today. She comes from England.'

Yves Grandet smiled and held out his hand towards Alyssa. 'I am so glad to meet you, Alyssa…may I call you Alyssa? You look about the same age as my daughter.'

Alyssa smiled back, and as they shook hands she formed an instant rapport with this small, rotund, friendly man.

The orthopaedic consultant turned to look at the X-ray screen, his face taking on a serious expression as he pointed out the various sections of the injury.

'Some of these little fragments of bone aren't going to be viable,' he murmured thoughtfully. 'But until I've opened up the leg in Theatre I won't know exactly how I'm going to approach the problem. I may have to fuse the ankle here.'

'We have a theatre ready, if you're going to operate this

evening, Yves,' Pierre offered. 'Or Henri could have his leg fixed on a back slab for the night. We could keep him well sedated and you could operate in the morning. The neurologist has checked our patient and reported that there is no damage to the cervical spine.'

'I'd prefer to operate this evening,' Yves said quickly. 'I'll go up and start getting ready for Theatre. I need to see that everything is exactly how I want it. Nurse! Yes, you!'

A startled young nurse hurried over.

'Come with me. I have a long list of things for my creature comforts before I start operating: a bottle of pure mineral water, some biscuits, very plain...'

Pierre smiled at Alyssa. 'Yves is always like this before a lengthy operation. And I think we both appreciate that this operation will take a long time.'

Alyssa nodded. 'That's what I was thinking.'

Pierre stood looking down at her, his eyes far too tender for her to feel easy about the situation.

'I've got a meeting in a few minutes.'

'I'll stay with Henri until the orthopaedic staff take over,' she said quietly.

'Thanks.' He hesitated. 'Good to have you on board, Alyssa.'

'It's good to be here.'

She watched as he turned and walked away.

Yes, she could handle this unnatural situation. The old days were over. This was a completely new situation. It wasn't going to be easy, but she wouldn't give in so long as she kept her emotions under control.

Easier said than done!

CHAPTER TWO

WHEN she first opened her eyes, Alyssa couldn't remember where she was. This wasn't her bedroom in east London. There was the steady hum of a city in the background, but outside her window the immediate sounds were different. Light was filtering through the curtains of her little room, trying to make sense of ill-defined objects and furniture, but Alyssa still felt completely disorientated.

Then she remembered. She was here in Paris, back at the *clinique* where it had all started, where her life had taken on a new meaning one wonderful summertime until, so agonisingly, her dreams of a perfect future had shattered.

She propped herself up against the pillows as she looked out towards the garden. There was no sound of activity in the garden this morning. Poor Henri would be lying in bed after his operation. She hoped it had been successful. You could never tell at this early stage. Orthopaedics was a slow business, and a great deal of patience was necessary by both patient and medical staff alike.

Lowering her feet to the floor, Alyssa felt the first chill of the morning as she walked barefoot from the bedside rug over the woodblock floor to the tiny *cabinet de toilette*. The heating from the radiator was beginning to make its presence felt, but it was obvious that winter was just around the corner.

As the hot water from the shower cascaded over her she felt her tense, tired body relaxing. Yesterday had been a long day. Getting here from England and meeting up with

Pierre again had been emotionally exhausting. Was she glad she'd come back to the *clinique*? Had it been a wise move?

She stepped out of the shower and reached for the *clinique* issue towel. Soft, fluffy and luxurious. The *clinique* never stinted on expense. Yes, she was glad she'd come back here. But, no, it hadn't been a wise move!

Rubbing herself vigorously with the towel, she remembered the number of times in the night when she'd awakened and tried to put Pierre from her mind so that she could sleep. But the image of his handsome, expressive face was always there to haunt her.

Alyssa went back into the bedroom and reached down into the depths of her still unpacked suitcase. Her new black suit would make her feel professional again.

Looking at herself in the mirror, she was pleasantly surprised. Yes, with the addition of her white silk blouse she looked efficient, professional—as if she *wasn't* scared stiff of people wondering all the time whether she was a proper doctor. Being small had its disadvantages, but she should have got used to it by now. In her social life it didn't make a scrap of difference, but in professional situations where everybody—patients and medical colleagues alike—towered over her, she longed to have a few extra inches of leg.

She gave a vigorous brush to her still damp blonde hair, glad that she'd let the hairdresser cut it short enough to be easily manageable. It had just the faintest hint of a wave which made the style less severe as it framed her face.

She told herself that so long as she did her job to her own satisfaction that was all that mattered. Well, perhaps not all that mattered. She also had to keep her emotions under control. Maybe she wouldn't have to see too much of Pierre. She had mixed feelings about that. Half of her wanted to avoid him whilst the other half, the wayward, wanton, emotional half, yearned to be with him every minute of the day.

Picking up her stethoscope, she opened the door and went out into the corridor, hoping that she could still find her way to the medical staff room. They served an excellent cup of black coffee, as she recalled.

Down on the ground floor, she found that the location of the staff room hadn't changed. When she pushed open the door the aroma of coffee assailed her nostrils. Mmm! She headed over to the serving counter, which was always referred to as the bar. A pleasant, diminutive middle-aged waitress in black dress and small white apron asked Alyssa what she would like.

'*Un petit café noir, s'il vous plaît,*' Alyssa replied.

'Ah, *mademoiselle*! I remember you!' The waitress leaned forward across the bar to shake hands with Alyssa. 'The little English girl. You were here a long time ago. You haven't changed at all. *Toujours petite!*'

Alyssa smiled. 'No, I haven't grown, Christine.'

She picked up the small cup of coffee. Nothing had changed here either.

She turned around to look for a table. And that was when she saw Pierre, seated by the window, looking out over the garden. He hadn't seen her. She ought to sit down at this table by the bar, pretend she hadn't...

Too late. As if drawn by the same magnetism that propelled her, Pierre turned and automatically raised his hand when he saw her, indicating that she should join him. Her heart began beating rapidly, but she allowed the magnetic force to move her across the room.

'*Bonjour, Alyssa. Tu as bien dormi?*'

Pierre was standing up in his gallant way, waiting for her to be seated before he resumed his own seat. Asking

Alyssa if she'd slept well was merely a customary morning greeting between friends or acquaintances. If he only knew how he'd been responsible for her lack of sleep!

She wouldn't enlighten him. Alyssa merely said that yes, she had slept well, and she took her place at the other side of the small, round, wooden table.

'No one working in the garden today?' she remarked, looking out of the window. 'Have you heard how Henri is?'

'Yes, Yves phoned me just before midnight to say that he was pleased with the outcome of the operation but the next few days will be critical. It was a difficult operation. Due to the pressure from the talus bone, which had been pushed up into the tibia in the impact of the fall, the tibia had shattered into more than twenty pieces. Yves had difficulty fixing them into position. Some of the smaller pieces of bone were completely unviable—as he thought.'

Alyssa nodded. 'So, did Yves have to do a complete reconstruction of the ankle?'

'Yes, he had to put in a steel plate and nail the bones into a viable position; he's hoping that there will still be some mobility in the ankle. He's put a plaster on the leg from below the knee, but left a window in the plaster so that we can keep a constant check on the wound.'

Alyssa took a sip of her coffee. 'That's always a good idea. Where there's an extensive wound such as Henri has we need to know how the healing process is progressing. And there's always the problem of a secondary infection in the post-operative stage.'

Pierre was watching her with a questioning expression on his face. 'I know you're interested in this case, so I thought you'd like to start work on the orthopaedic floor. As you probably gathered when you were here last time, our doctors have to work in all areas of the hospital and we call in specialists from other hospitals to advise or perform surgical operations when required. Last night you expressed an interest in orthopaedics, and also in obstetrics and gynaecology, so—'

'I'm quite happy to work wherever you think I would be most—'

'I'd like you to have the opportunity to work in obstetrics and gynaecology after you've had a short spell in orthopaedics,' Pierre continued, as if Alyssa hadn't interrupted.

Alyssa took a deep breath. Somehow she didn't think working with babies was going to be such a good idea if Pierre was likely to be anywhere in the same building. But in her contract she had agreed to work wherever she was assigned.

'Well, you're the *médecin-chef*,' she said lightly.

A shadow passed over Pierre's face. 'Do I gather that you would prefer to stay in orthopaedics? I thought you liked working with babies.'

'As I said, both orthopaedics and obstetrics are extremely interesting,' Alyssa said evenly. 'That was one of the things that drew me to working here at the *clinique*. The opportunity to move around from one area to the other. I enjoy being versatile in my work. It's so different to London, where I had to commit to—'

She broke off as she saw the hardened expression on Pierre's face.

'You don't like to commit yourself, do you, Alyssa?' Pierre murmured. 'Keep moving. That seems to be your philosophy.'

She could feel a lump in her throat. She longed to be able to tell Pierre why she hadn't been able to commit to a lasting relationship with him, but she knew she had to keep up the charade.

'It works very well for me,' she said, in a false, facetious tone, hating the image she was portraying.

'I'm sure it does,' Pierre said evenly.

'And how about you, Pierre? Have you made any strong commitments since I last saw you?'

'If you mean the ultimate commitment of marriage, then the answer's no,' he replied smoothly. 'I've had a few affairs since we last met but...but no. *Je suis toujours célibataire.*'

Alyssa ran a hand through her short blonde hair. 'I'm not sure *célibataire* is the right word. I know it's the French word for bachelor, but I wouldn't imagine you've remained celibate.'

Pierre raised an eyebrow. 'Did you expect me to remain celibate after we parted?'

Alyssa pushed back her chair and stood up. Whatever kind of conversation she and Pierre enjoyed, it would always turn to their previous relationship. They'd shared so much together. It was hard trying to be just good friends.

'I'm going to the bar to get a croissant.'

Pierre was already on his feet. 'I'll get it.' He moved swiftly to take her by the arm. 'Sit down again, Alyssa. We haven't finished our discussion about your work role here.'

Reluctantly she sat down, telling herself she must remain unemotional until they'd finished their conversation. No more references to the past. No more questions about how they'd lived during the past eight years of separation. Like hers, Pierre's private life had to remain private if they were to survive until after Christmas.

The thought of Christmas in Paris would have excited her so much if she and Pierre had still been lovers. She remembered how they'd always walked hand in hand beside the Seine, looking into the swirling waters, discussing anything and everything…and how much they loved simply being together…

He was returning to the table. She put on a bright smile and assumed her role of platonic friend, chiding herself for her momentary lapse from her assumed character.

'Christine is bringing over our *petit déjeuner*,' Pierre said. 'She insisted.'

Alyssa smiled. 'One of the perks of being the *médecin-chef.*'

Pierre smiled back and Alyssa felt her heart lift as she saw the way his facial features lit up in that interesting and expressive way when he was happy. This was the Pierre she remembered. Carefree, looking forward to the future.

'Yes, there are advantages to being the boss,' Pierre said lightly.

Christine was now setting out croissants, bread, butter and apricot jam on the table.

'Christine remembers me when I was a young doctor here, one of many—don't you, Christine?' Pierre looked up at the waitress with a whimsical smile.

'You haven't changed, *monsieur.*' Christine patted Pierre's shoulder affectionately before returning to her work behind the bar.

Pierre looked across the table at Alyssa. 'Oh, but I have changed,' he said meaningfully. 'I'm not half as trusting as I used to be. I never take anything for granted.'

Alyssa broke off a piece of flaky croissant and spread it with apricot jam. When she raised her eyes she saw that Pierre was still looking at her.

'That's called experience,' she said quietly. 'Life is a learning curve. You learn from what happens to you, then leave all that baggage behind and move on.'

'Move on?' he repeated softly. 'Is that what you're doing, Alyssa? Then why have you come back here?'

'Good question,' she said slowly, playing for time until she could compose her thoughts into some kind of order. 'I suppose I felt there was some unfinished business here. I had to completely lay the ghost.'

Pierre leaned back against his chair, putting both hands behind his head as he eyed her with a puzzled frown. 'Is that what I was? A ghost?'

'Oh, you know what I mean. It's just an English expression. It means to get rid of the past…of the baggage from the past… Oh, I don't know—stop twisting my words.'

An amused smile was hovering on Pierre's lips. 'So I can choose whether I want to be called a ghost or a piece of baggage, can I?'

'Oh, Pierre!' Alyssa brought her hand down on the table in exasperation. 'You know what I mean…'

Pierre leaned across the table and took hold of her hand, bringing his face oh, so tantalisingly close to hers. The faint scent of his aftershave was causing havoc with her emotions. She remembered this cologne so well—it was the one he'd applied to his body after a particularly exciting shower they'd taken together. And then he'd applied it to both of them, and…

'Just teasing!' he whispered.

Alyssa realised that the room had gone quiet. The medical staff enjoying their *petit déjeuner* were all looking across at the newly appointed *médecin-chef* with his English friend, whose role at the *clinique* had yet to be defined.

Alyssa decided to ignore the curious looks as she wallowed in Pierre's attention. A girl could drown in those dark brown expressive eyes!

'You always did like to tease me,' she said softly. 'But in those days I knew how to handle it. Now…'

She took her hand from his grip and leaned back in her chair, putting a safe distance between them.

'Now the situation is different,' she said, half under her breath, as she tried to bring her emotions under control.

'Yes, the situation is different.' Pierre took a sip of his coffee. 'We are…how do you say it in English?…we are just good friends. And so, as just good friends, I wondered if you would like to come out to the theatre with me this evening. I bought a couple of theatre tickets last week, hoping I could persuade some beautiful unattached young lady to accompany me.'

Alyssa could feel her spirits lifting. Pierre was certainly playing along with her charade now, and the thought of an innocuous, no strings attached evening with him was exciting.

'I'd love to go to the theatre…that is unless the *médecin-chef* asks me to work this evening.'

Pierre smiled. 'Oh, I don't think he would be so hard-hearted as to prevent a young lady going out to see the bright lights of Paris after her first full day here. After all, the *médecin-chef* knows he must keep his staff happy. Some members of staff like to have a quiet night in, but others, like yourself, prefer to… How do you say it in English? Go out on the town? Yes, that's what you like to do, isn't it, Alyssa?'

He was standing up now, the smile still on his face as he looked down at her. 'I'd like to take you along to the orthopaedic unit now. Yves Grandet is calling in to see how Henri is after last night's operation. He's asked the orthopaedic team to meet him up there, so if you come along with me now I could introduce you to the staff and—'

'Pierre? Before we go up to the orthopaedic ward I...'

Alyssa stood up but still found herself craning her neck as she looked upwards towards the lofty Pierre. Yes, she was anxious to get started on her work here, but Pierre's quip about the bright lights was still stinging. How little he knew about her real self! About what she really wanted in life. But she couldn't enlighten him. She had to go on playing the role she'd set herself.

'Yes?' he asked, waiting to hear what she had to say.

'Oh...er...what time shall we meet tonight?'

'I'll meet you in the foyer of the *clinique* at seven. We can have a drink somewhere before the play starts.'

They walked in silence to the end of the corridor. Pierre pressed the button which would summon the lift. They waited a couple of minutes, still maintaining an awkward silence. Nothing happened.

Pierre tapped his fingers against the wall impatiently. 'I think there must be a problem with the lift. We'll have to use the stairs.'

As they mounted the stairs side by side Pierre found difficulty in maintaining a reasonable space between them. He was longing to reach out and take hold of her hand, as he would have done in the days long ago when they were lovers, but he knew if he reached out and showed his true feelings the possibility of friendship would be dashed.

With an effort he concentrated his thoughts on the work ahead of them. Alyssa's interest in orthopaedics had surprised him. He'd been sure she would have preferred obstetrics, from what they had discussed the last time she was here. Orthopaedics required physical strength—and, with the greatest will in the world, you only had to look at Alyssa to know that physical strength wouldn't be her strong point.

He glanced down at her now and caught her eye.

She looked up and gave him a nervous smile. 'Do the staff of the orthopaedic ward know I'm coming in today?'

'Don't worry, they won't bite you, Alyssa. The sister in charge of the ward, Sylvie, is a great friend of mine. If you'd been unable to go to the theatre this evening I would have asked her.'

Somehow that didn't make Alyssa feel any happier!

'It's a purely platonic friendship, of course,' Pierre said lightly.

'Of course.'

'Just like our friendship is now, Alyssa.'

Her pulse quickened. 'Don't tease me, Pierre. You know that friendship between a couple who've been lovers can never be truly platonic. There's always that underlying factor that has to be stamped out. Or perhaps...' She hesitated. 'Perhaps you and Sylvie have been lovers?'

She held her breath. It was much too bold a question, and quite out of character, but she knew she would find it difficult to work with someone who had experienced an affair with Pierre.

Pierre's eyes flashed dangerously. 'No, we haven't. Not that it's any business of yours.' He paused, running a hand through his dark hair with long, sensitive fingers. 'But if you're going to ask personal questions like that, then so am I. Is there any special person waiting for you back in England?'

Alyssa was relieved that her London life was now so uncomplicated that she could be utterly truthful with Pierre. She smiled across at him.

'Only my cat, who's being looked after by a neighbour.'

Pierre smiled back. 'Cats are incredibly independent creatures. Rather like you. I'm not surprised you have a cat as a companion.'

They had reached the top step and Pierre decided that he dared put a hand under Alyssa's arm to steady her.

As Alyssa paused to regain her breath, she looked up at Pierre, willing herself not to be too unnerved by the touch of his fingers under her elbow. His comment about her not needing anybody was still stinging. She couldn't let it pass. Pierre had to know that she was still human.

'I had a husband once,' she said quietly.

She realised almost at once that she was in danger of blowing her cover by mentioning Mike.

Pierre stared down into her eyes with that piercing appraisal she remembered so well, as if he was looking right inside her soul. Surely if she told him now that she couldn't have babies, and that was why she'd had to break off their— No! She mustn't! She'd got this far, and their new platonic relationship would work out if she kept her cool.

'You had a husband?' His voice was low. 'What happened? Was it one of those totally free marriages where each partner goes their own way and—?'

'Don't, Pierre!' She pulled free from the constriction of his hand. 'You wouldn't understand.'

'Oh, but I think I would!' He took a deep breath. 'I don't want to pry. Especially not here at the *clinique*. We owe it to the patients to remain calm, and if either of us becomes emotional…'

The sound of footsteps resounding on the corridor made Alyssa nervous of the situation. 'Let's leave it, Pierre. We can talk tonight.'

Pierre pulled himself to his full height and began to move away, indicating that Alyssa should follow him. He was once more the eminent *médecin-chef*, pausing briefly to reply *'Bonjour,'* to the white-uniformed nurse who greeted him in the corridor.

They reached the orthopaedic ward and Pierre pushed open the swing doors.

Alyssa took a deep breath as she followed him through. She wasn't normally nervous when coming on duty, but this morning was different. This morning she had to give a good impression to the nursing staff, who would want to feel they could trust her skills and knowledge.

Pierre headed for the room where their patient Henri was settled back against his pillows, with his injured right leg propped up high on a special orthopaedic cradle.

The small, plump figure of the orthopaedic consultant, wearing a dark suit this morning, was surrounded by what looked like a positive crowd of doctors, nurses and medical students. He was bending over the leg, adjusting the angle of a drainage tube.

One of the medical students was pointing out the size of the consultant's posterior as his back was turned towards them.

Medical students never change! Alyssa thought, hiding a smile. It was amazing how they turned into capable doctors.

She scanned the faces of Yves Grandet's entourage and was pleased to recognise someone she knew. Jacques Suchet, the friendly young fair-haired doctor who'd carried her suitcase up the steps yesterday, smiled across at her. She smiled back. It was good to know she already had a friend on the orthopaedic team.

'*Bonjour, Yves,*' Pierre said to the consultant.

Yves smiled as he straightened up and turned round. '*Bonjour, Pierre—et bonjour, Alyssa.*'

Alyssa smiled as she returned the greeting. She liked this friendly consultant very much already. He exuded the confidence and capability of a highly successful surgeon whilst remaining very down to earth and approachable.

'It was important I call in on my way to another hospital, to check on my very special patient,' Yves said, addressing his medical colleagues in the tone of voice he adopted when giving lectures. 'I don't like to spend hours operating on a patient who doesn't behave himself, and I felt Henri might pose a problem.'

Their patient knew he was joking, and smiled around at the assembled medical staff. The consultant leaned across and patted Henri on the shoulder.

'But I'm glad to say that Henri is being a perfect patient so far. Apart from running too high a temperature, he's doing fine. I'm going to put all of you in the picture so that you can take good care of Henri when I'm not here.' He glanced at his watch. 'I'll be brief, because I have to be on the other side of Paris in an hour.'

Alyssa studied her patient's leg, taking in the full details of the case as Yves outlined the operation he'd performed. It was much as Pierre had already explained to her when they were having their *petit déjeuner*.

'So, I think intravenous antibiotics should be continued,' Yves was saying, in conclusion of his instructions. 'The high temperature is worrying at this stage. Because of the open wound there is a high risk of infection.'

'Has a swab been taken from the wound for histology?' Alyssa asked, examining the area where the surgical incision had been sutured through the window in the rigid plaster.

'That's all under control,' said a quiet composed voice as the sister in charge of the orthopaedic ward stepped forward. 'We are expecting results from the pathology laboratory this morning.'

'I'd like to know the results as soon as they come in, Sylvie,' Pierre said, giving her an approving smile.

Sylvie smiled back and the rapport between the two wasn't lost on Alyssa.

Alyssa looked across at the dark-haired, blue-uniformed sister, and her first impression was one of a young woman who was extremely competent, devoted to her job, highly efficient…and with long, slim legs that seemed to go up to her armpits!

Alyssa told herself to concentrate on the task in hand and not allow jealousy to get in the way of caring for the patient.

'We can close up the window in the plaster now,' Yves said. 'The wound should remain covered as much as possible, but nevertheless we need to keep an eye on it.'

After Yves had gone, Pierre introduced Alyssa to the rest of the orthopaedic team.

'Pierre, would you like me to show Dr Ferguson round the orthopaedic ward?' Sylvie asked. 'I know you must have a million other things to do.'

'Thank you, Sylvie, that would be very helpful.' Pierre turned to look down at Alyssa. 'I'll leave you in Sister's capable hands.'

He moved away quickly and left the unit.

Alyssa looked around her, feeling decidedly apprehensive about her new job.

'This way, Dr Ferguson, *s'il vous plaît*,' Sylvie was saying.

Alyssa felt completely dwarfed as she walked beside the tall sister, but as the ward round continued she found she was enjoying herself. It was good to be working again, and she enjoyed meeting the patients and checking up on their case notes, which were all attached in folders to the foot of the beds. It was a mixed ward to the extent that some bays were female, others male, and there was freedom to move around for the more ambulant patients, which, meant that they didn't get too bored with their incarceration.

Alyssa found Sylvie was extremely helpful and thorough in her explanation of the treatment the patients were undergoing. She told Alyssa that very few patients were confined to bed. The policy on the ward was to get the patients moving as soon as possible, even if it meant they had to walk around with heavy steel fixators in their limbs to keep the bones in place.

Patients who had extreme difficulty with walking were given wheelchairs, so that they could circulate amongst the other patients or even take the lift down to the ground floor and go out into the garden.

'Dr Ferguson, this is Jean-Claude,' Sylvie said, as the two of them were almost mown down by an enthusiastic young man speeding his wheelchair away from one of the bays. 'He thinks he's a racing driver so you'd better be careful when he's out of bed.'

'Sorry, Sylvie!' Jean Claude called out as he whizzed off in the opposite direction from them. 'Didn't see you!'

'He's a cheerful patient.' Alyssa smiled. 'What's his diagnosis, Sister?'

'He was climbing in the Pyrenees when he fell down a rockface and cut his leg. A local doctor put stitches in. The wound healed over but after a few months Jean-Claude's leg became very painful. Yves Grandet operated to open up the leg and discovered extensive gangrene in the lower part of the tibia. Years ago he would have had to have a below-knee amputation, but Yves was able to excise the affected part of the bone and replace it with a steel rod.'

'Has he had plastic surgery to cover the wound?' Alyssa asked.

Sylvie nodded. 'The front part of the steel rod has been covered with a flap of flesh and skin, but the posterior part will need further treatment to make the steel rod less visible. We're liaising with the plastic surgery team about a future date for further surgery—'

Sylvie broke off and smiled down at Alyssa. 'You've probably seen enough of the patients for the moment. Now that you know your way around you'll find all the information you need in the notes, and you can always ask the rest of the team. Would you like to come and have coffee with me in the office, Dr Ferguson?'

'I'd love to—and do call me Alyssa.'

Sylvie pushed open the door of her office. 'And you must call me Sylvie. Everybody does. We don't stand on ceremony at the Clinique Ste Catherine. Our *médecin chef* is calm and relaxed about protocol and I'm pleased that Pierre hasn't changed anything now he's taken over. How do you find Pierre?'

Momentarily, the question threw her. Alyssa had no idea how she was going to reply as she sat down near Sylvie's desk. Watching her new colleague as she poured strong coffee from a *cafetière* into two tiny cups, she thought how different this was from the mugs of instant coffee she was used to in her London hospital. But then, this was Paris.

As the ward sister handed her one of the cups Alyssa couldn't help wondering just how platonic *was* this friendship that Sylvie and Pierre were having? And how much did Sylvie know about her own previous relationship with Pierre?

'I only arrived yesterday,' Alyssa said, playing safe. 'So I haven't had much time to—'

'Yes, in spite of his friendliness, it takes time to get to know Pierre,' Sylvie said. 'I've been out with him a few times, but even though we are friends I still don't feel I know much about him.'

Alyssa stiffened.

'I mean, he's such a handsome, intriguing man!' Sylvie went on enthusiastically, her rapid French breaking into Alyssa's thoughts. *'Ça m'étonne qu'il est toujours célibataire!'*

'Yes, it is surprising that he's still a bachelor,' Alyssa said, echoing Sylvie's words. 'But—'

'It's just impossible to get close to him—and he doesn't talk about his past relationships. He's told me about his wonderful life in the West Indies, but there's something lacking in his emotions. It's as if— *Excusez-moi…*'

Sylvie broke off to answer her phone.

'Oui…j'arrive tout de suite.'

Sylvie put the phone down and stood up. 'I've got to go back on the ward, Alyssa. *A tout à l'heure.* I'll see you later. And don't forget—if I can be of any help while you're working here…'

Sylvie swept out of the door, leaving Alyssa feeling that she should have broken through the flow of Sylvie's enthusiastic description of Pierre to explain her own previous relationship with him.

She put down her coffee cup and stood up. She would go round the patients once more, to familiarise herself with all the current treatments, and she would go back to see the young woman who'd complained that the site around the intravenous canula in her hand was painful. The patient had been on intravenous antibiotics for over a week now, so it looked as if a change of canula into the other hand was indicated.

Work always took her mind away from her problems, she thought as she went back into the ward. Tonight, when she was once more with Pierre, would be time enough to consider whether she could handle this new platonic relationship.

CHAPTER THREE

ALYSSA paused at the end of the corridor as she looked across the foyer at the handsome stranger who was waiting to take her out that evening. In reality, Pierre wasn't a stranger, but the eight years they'd been apart had caused a rift wider than the widest canyon. A rift that neither of them must cross. Tonight they must be platonic friends having a date in the most wonderful city in the world.

Pierre hadn't seen her yet. He was standing with his back to the reception desk, looking out towards the large plate glass windows where the twinkling lights of Paris were illuminating the darkness of this chilly November evening. Soon the whole of Paris would be lit up with Christmas decorations. Frosted illuminations would span the wide boulevards like fairy bridges and excited shoppers would gather round the enticing displays of Christmas presents in the windows of the shops and little boutiques.

Alyssa felt a sense of apprehensive anticipation as she thought about the impending Christmas season and all it had meant to her in the past. What would this Christmas bring now that she had met up again with Pierre? She felt her heart beating rapidly as she watched him by the window. He was wearing a dark grey suit, impeccably tailored to fit his lean, athletic figure. She guessed that he hadn't put on even half a kilo in the eight years they'd been apart.

She was trying desperately to get a hold on her emotions, but all she could feel was an overwhelming desire to rush across and fling herself into Pierre's arms. And the way she was feeling at the moment made her want to suggest to him that they cancel the theatre date and stay in tonight, just the two of them, so that...

He turned and saw her. She felt the most annoyingly telling blush spreading across her cheeks. How long did she have to keep up this pretence? Pierre had said he was in charge here until just after Christmas. Could she hold out that long without giving in to her turbulent desires?

Pierre smiled and his face lit up with pleasure as he came towards her.

'Ah, there you are. How did you get on today? We haven't lost any patients, so I presume you've been making yourself useful.'

Alyssa stiffened as she felt his hand gliding under her elbow to guide her towards the revolving door. Outside on the steps he paused, standing back so that he could take a better look at her.

'You're looking lovely tonight, Alyssa. Am I allowed to say that, now that we're just good friends?'

She ran a hand through her short blonde hair, still damp from the shower, and wondered if Pierre realised how long she'd agonised over what to wear. Deciding on this cream woollen skirt and jacket had been a major decision, despite how many times she'd told herself she wasn't supposed to be trying to impress Pierre.

'Oh, I'm happy to receive compliments,' Alyssa said, smiling up at Pierre, his face so familiar but so untouchable now.

She swung into step beside him as they walked along the road.

'We'll get a taxi at the corner here,' Pierre said. 'The traffic is pretty dense, but eventually we'll get there.'

'Why don't we take the Métro, like we always used...?' Alyssa's voice trailed away as nostalgic emotions threatened to get the better of her. She mustn't keep referring to their previous life together.

Pierre looked surprised. 'I thought now that you were more sophisticated you would prefer to take a taxi.'

'I'm eight years older but I'm no more "sophisticated" than I was when we last met,' Alyssa said quietly. 'I like taking the Métro. It's always nice and warm down there, and it's usually quicker when the traffic's bad.'

As they walked along the Avenue Mozart Alyssa paused briefly to admire the Christmas-themed window of one of the shops where her grandmother had often taken her as a child. A small tinsel-draped Father Christmas was standing with his elves and reindeer amid the cheeses and hams.

Pierre raised one eyebrow. 'A bit premature to start the Christmas decorations in November, don't you think, Alyssa?'

She smiled. 'Not at all. Christmas will soon be here, and it catches everyone by surprise if we're not reminded to start getting ready. It's pure nostalgia for me, and it makes me feel I'm very young again.'

Pierre laughed. 'You *are* young, Alyssa.'

They made for the Ranelagh Métro station, which was the nearest, and ran down the steps. Pierre produced a couple of tickets from his *carnet*, the book of tickets in his pocket, and they went through the *guichet* to the platform.

'It's a long time since we were on this station together,' Pierre said, in a voice smoothly devoid of emotion.

'I was thinking that,' Alyssa said, deliberately focusing her eyes on the advertisement posters plastered over the walls.

'I remember exactly when it was,' Pierre said, his voice husky with emotion. 'Don't you?'

Alyssa steeled herself for the nostalgic experience he would inevitably conjure up.

'I think so,' she said carefully, knowing full well the wonderful evening Pierre was referring to.

Pierre smiled. 'We took the Métro over to the Rive Gauche, as I recall, and had supper in that little café overlooking the river. The one where the waiter always used to try and listen in to our conversation. And afterwards we came back here and—'

'It's all so long ago,' Alyssa cut in quickly, before Pierre had time to refer to that night of pure magic, her last night in Paris, the night before she'd gone back to London to continue her studies at medical school and then discovered that she was pregnant—only to lose the most precious baby in the world.

'Yes,' Pierre said softly. 'Difficult to believe it all happened. I've often wondered if…'

The roar of the Métro train approaching drowned his words. Alyssa climbed aboard, trying to remain calm when her shoulder was pressed against Pierre's side as they sat together. Physical contact with someone you loved desperately was an unnerving experience which threatened to blow away all her resolutions not to revive their previous relationship.

'I've often wondered if things would have been different between us if you'd stayed on in Paris.'

Pierre was looking sideways at her as he resumed what he'd been going to say before.

'You mean, if I'd given up my medical studies?'

'No, if you'd perhaps taken a year out to think about the situation. Maybe I pressurised you too much into the idea of marriage. You were very young, after all, and you—'

'Pierre, it wouldn't have made any difference to the situation,' Alyssa said, hating herself for not being able to explain the real reason. 'I was… Circumstances change, and I felt that marriage to you wasn't the right thing.'

'So you married someone else.'

Alyssa could hear the deep emotion in Pierre's voice and it tore at her heartstrings. No wonder Sylvie had said she couldn't get close to him. Pierre was a man whose heart had been broken by her own refusal to marry him. And he was still carrying the scars.

'Yes, I did marry someone else, but—'

'We get out here,' Pierre said, putting out a hand to help her rise from her seat.

Amid the noise and the crowds as they emerged into the busy street it was impossible to continue. Pierre's arm was comfortingly on the small of her back as they negotiated a path through a group of lively young students to secure a table outside a small café. An overhead heater was dispelling the November chill in the air and the bright lights from the theatre opposite were creating a carnival atmosphere, reminiscent of the balmy summer evening when they'd last been here. That had been another momentous occasion, almost as poignant in retrospect as her last evening in Paris.

Alyssa looked at Pierre across the small wrought-iron table, with its red and white checked tablecloth, and her heart felt as if it would burst if she had to keep a hold on her emotions much longer.

'You shouldn't have brought me here…to this café…to this table,' she said, her voice quivering with feeling as she remembered how they'd come here so often—holding hands across the table, feeling the electric current passing from fingertip to fingertip, until it had consumed their entire bodies and they'd had to hurry back to Pierre's apartment so that they could consummate their love once more.

He feigned surprise. 'Why not? I thought you liked it here.'

'I do, but…'

'You were telling me about your husband, remember?' he said evenly. 'What I can't understand is how you could tell me that you were dead against marriage and then off you go—'

'Like I said, situations change,' she interrupted quickly. 'I'd finished my final exams; I'd qualified as a doctor. Mike was a fellow medical student, a good friend who qualified at the same time, and we started going out together. We got on well…and it seemed like a good idea to get married.'

It sounded lame even to her own ears. She would have to come up with something better. But, whatever she told Pierre, she wasn't going to say that she'd found she couldn't bear a lifetime of loneliness and that one of the other reasons she'd felt she could marry Mike was because he'd said he didn't want a family.

He had, in fact, been completely against the idea of having babies when they'd first married. He had said he didn't even like children and felt that family would just get in the way of his career. So when Alyssa had told Mike, before she'd agreed to marry him, that she probably couldn't have a baby, it hadn't affected him in the slightest. He'd seemed relieved.

That had been at the beginning of their marriage. But two years later, Mike had changed his mind completely out of the blue and had announced that he'd like a family after all.

For two years they'd tried for a baby, but Alyssa hadn't got pregnant. And it had been at that point that Mike told her he was having an affair, his girlfriend was pregnant and he was going to go and live with her.

Pierre leaned across the table. 'You're looking very solemn all of a sudden. From the way you're reacting there doesn't seem to have been much romance in this marriage.'

'Oh, it had its moments.'

She swallowed hard as she tried to remember if she'd ever really fallen in love with Mike and came to the conclusion that she hadn't realised that it would be impossible to get over Pierre. No wonder Mike had left her! She'd only had half a heart to give him, and after the heartbreaking two years of trying to get pregnant, she had accepted that she was childless. As friends they'd got on well; as married partners it had been a disaster.

She raised her eyes to Pierre's and saw her own deep sadness reflected there. Why did they have to torture each other like this? Why couldn't it be like it was before she lost their baby?

Because that's life, said the still, small voice of reason. You have to take the good times with the bad and make the best of it. You can't change the fact that you can't give Pierre a baby, so it wouldn't be fair to marry him.

The waiter was placing their drinks on the table. A pastis for Pierre and a kir made from crème de cassis and white wine for Alyssa. Nothing has changed as far as our drinks are concerned, she thought, as she watched Pierre pouring water from the little jug into his glass, making it cloudy.

'Who broke up the marriage?' Pierre asked quietly.

'Mike left me…for my best friend, Rachel. She was one of our theatre sisters.'

'That must have been awful for you.'

'I'd realised that something was going on between them. I wasn't surprised.'

'But weren't you devastated?'

She weighed her words carefully. 'To be honest, I think

it was a relief. You see, we hadn't been getting on very well for some time so…'

She paused, unable to continue because of the way Pierre was looking at her.

'As far as I can see, first of all you drifted into a boring marriage with an unsuitable partner when you really didn't want to get married anyway. And then, having found out the situation was awful, you weren't sad when it all ended and you could go back to your exciting life as an independent bachelor girl.'

She took a larger sip of her drink and forced herself to smile. 'You sound like a psychiatrist who specialises in analysing marriage break-ups.'

'Do I? OK, if that's how it looks to you,' he said, placing his elbow on the table and one hand at the side of his face as he leaned over. 'But tell me, Alyssa, do you think you will you ever try marriage again?'

She took a deep breath. 'What do you think?'

'I thought not. But all men aren't like your unfortunate Mike, you know.'

She wanted to tell Pierre that most men wanted to have a family, and that was something she couldn't give to anyone. But she simply remained silent.

Instead she leaned forward. 'Now it's your turn to tell me what *you've* been doing for the past eight years.'

Pierre remained silent for a few seconds as he contemplated just how much he should tell Alyssa. The main problem since they'd split up had been his efforts to forget her. Just when he thought he'd got Alyssa out of his system, something would happen to remind him of her and he would be back to square one again. But he wasn't going to mention any of this.

'I've got this fabulous house on the island of Ste Cécile in the West Indies. Fully staffed, of course. All the domestic side of work is taken care of, so I spend my off-duty time on the sea. I love taking friends out on my boat, exploring the coastline, picnicking under the palm trees on the beach—'

He broke off and smiled across the table at Alyssa. Was he painting too alluring a picture for her? Was he trying too hard to convince her that he enjoyed life without her?

Alyssa smiled back. 'It sounds idyllic. No special girl-friend, then? I thought you would have married by now, knowing how you long to have a family.'

Pierre drew in his breath. 'A family is still my dearest wish,' he said, his voice husky. 'I was an only child, an adopted child…but I believe I told you this when you were here in Paris last time, didn't I?'

'Yes, you did,' Alyssa said quietly. 'I remember you said that you wanted to have your own flesh and blood around you, to create a Dupont dynasty. Being adopted yourself, you were determined to have a real family of your own.'

'Did I say that? What a brilliant memory you have, Alyssa.'

'Yes, it made a big impression on me. That's why I thought you would have made a start on your family by now.'

'Haven't met the right mother for my children yet—that is apart from…apart from one or two girls I thought I'd fallen for. But I was quickly disillusioned.'

'You're probably being too choosy,' Alyssa said lightly, assuming her role of platonic, carefree friend. 'Someone will come along and you'll immediately know she's right for you.'

Pierre swallowed hard and leaned across the table to take hold of Alyssa's hand. 'I hope so.'

Alyssa stared down at her hand, imprisoned in Pierre's.

Oh, the feel of his fingers was far too pleasurable! Carefully, she withdrew her hand and leaned back in her chair.

'Give it time, Pierre,' she said quietly.

They finished their drinks and crossed the road to the theatre. The noise of Paris night-life had always excited Alyssa, and tonight was no exception. Amid the busy traffic Pierre took hold of her hand, to lead her to the safety of the pavement, and she didn't try to pull away. This could only be construed as a friendly gesture, so she tried to ignore the frisson of desire that flickered through her at the touch of his fingers.

Alyssa enjoyed every moment of the play. She also enjoyed being escorted to the bar in the interval by the most handsome man in the theatre audience. They kept their conversation deliberately light, discussing the play, the plot, the actors and actresses.

'It's good for me to see a contemporary play in France,' Alyssa said, as she sipped her drink. 'My French needs updating. Back in London I rarely use it. Since my mother died I've spoken only English.'

'How long is it since your mother died?'

'It was my last year at medical school. I was living with her so that I could take care of her, and our house wasn't too far from the hospital or the medical school. About half an hour on the Underground. I continued to live at home after she died and took over the mortgage. Mike moved in with me when we married.'

'And your father? I remember you said he lived in Australia. Do you have any contact with him?'

Alyssa shook her head. 'Not since he left my mother when I was very small. Maman came over from Paris to be an au pair in her summer vacation from university. She met my father and he persuaded her to stay on in London.

She got pregnant with me and so they married. My father left home when I was about six months old.'

'You didn't tell me that before,' Pierre said softly.

'There's lots I haven't told you,' she said quietly, putting down her drink.

'The second half of the play is about to begin,' Pierre said, standing up and holding out his hand towards her.

Automatically, before she could think, she took hold of his hand, revelling in the feel of his fingers wrapping around her own. Walking hand in hand together into the auditorium couldn't do any harm…

The rapport between them was now palpable. However hard she tried, Alyssa was never going to be able to shake off her love for Pierre. She realised, not for the first time, that they were made for each other. They could try, but nothing was ever going to change that.

Pierre guided her through the crowded foyer at the end of the play and they walked down towards the Seine. The restaurant where Pierre had made a reservation was equally crowded, but the waiter showed them to a secluded corner table. Alyssa was relieved that this was a restaurant where they hadn't been before. Too much heart-rending nostalgia was wearing down her resolve.

'I don't remember ever having been here,' Alyssa said, settling herself on the banquette and looking up at the ornate alabaster ceiling which was punctuated with a myriad of tiny halogen lights. 'Very smart.'

Pierre smiled. 'I couldn't afford to bring you here in the old days. Way beyond my wallet then. I knew you'd be impressed with the place.'

Alyssa laughed. 'Is that why you brought me here? To impress me?'

'I bring all my girlfriends here,' he said, in a bantering tone.

'Well, they'd expect only the best restaurants from the *médecin-chef* of the prestigious Clinique Ste Catherine,' Alyssa said, in the same half-joking manner, although the thought of Pierre taking girlfriends anywhere was agonising in the extreme.

'You must try the *escargots*,' Pierre told her. 'They serve small portions as a starter and they are exquisitely cooked in garlic and butter.'

'Mmm…sounds great. Just like my grandmother used to cook them.'

'And their fish is magnificent. So fresh it—'

Pierre broke off to speak to the waiter who was going to take their order.

Alyssa sat back in her chair and watched him giving precise instructions. This had always happened when they'd had a meal together. They both got an idea of what they wanted to eat and rarely consulted the menu. Pierre was looking enquiringly across the table at her and she nodded, yes, to his question about whether she would like the sole *meunière*.

Of course she would like it, if that was what Pierre was recommending. Oh, dear, she was falling so easily back into the easy relationship they'd had. There was nothing platonic about the electric vibes that were crossing the table at the moment.

She sipped a glass of chilled white wine as she tried to still her turbulent emotions. Even in a completely new restaurant the nostalgic feelings followed them. They had too much history behind them to make a transition into the present and the unknown future.

As the meal progressed their conversation flowed easily—both of them now seeming to make an effort to avoid referring to the past. When they'd discussed this evening's play Pierre asked Alyssa about what was on in London at the moment. She was able to describe the theatres she'd been to most recently, and that was a completely safe subject.

Alyssa put down her coffee cup at the end of the meal and smiled across the table. 'That was superb.'

'Glad you enjoyed it. How about a liqueur?'

Now he really was being nostalgic! How many times had she sipped her favourite liqueur, with its piquant flavour of oranges, at the end of an evening with Pierre? But not tonight! That would be the ultimate undoing of all her resolutions. The white wine she'd drunk had already made her feel far too mellow towards Pierre, and too much off her guard.

'No, thanks,' she said quickly.

Pierre arched an eyebrow. 'That's unusual for you. I'm not trying to seduce you—I've got the message, you know. We're just good friends on a platonic night out. So you're quite safe if—' His mobile phone was shrilling. *'Allo? Oui, c'est Pierre Dupont içi…'*

Pierre was looking serious now. Alyssa drained her coffee cup. He seemed to be dealing with some kind of medical emergency. They were both off duty but Pierre, as director of the *clinique*, would often be consulted during his own time.

'Oui, j'arrive tout de suite,' he said tersely, before cutting the connection.

'What's the problem, Pierre?'

He was standing up, signalling to the waiter to bring the bill.

'A multiple pile-up on the Périphérique. All hospitals in Paris are on alert and we've been asked to take some casualties at the *clinique*.'

Outside on the pavement, Pierre was able to flag down a cab. The traffic had eased since the early pre-theatre rush.

She sat bolt upright next to him, aware of the tense atmosphere. The romantic ambience that had surrounded them all evening had dissipated at the realisation that they would have to become professionals again.

'I'll come into the *clinique* and work with you, if you need me,' Alyssa said, thinking that a multiple pile-up on the Périphérique, the fast-flowing ring-road that surrounded Paris, would be an extremely serious situation.

'Thanks, that would be a great help, Alyssa. Your experience and knowledge of orthopaedics will be useful. I'll phone Sylvie and see if she's available to come back and take charge of her ward. The night staff are very efficient, but Sylvie always likes to be on her ward if there's an emergency.'

Alyssa could hear Pierre speaking to Sylvie now. Yes, it sounded as if she was going to come in. And it also reaffirmed the fact that she and Pierre had a good relationship between them.

Alyssa tried to convince herself that she was glad about that, but failed miserably. She wanted Pierre to find someone he could be happy with. Someone who could give him the family he so desperately craved. But standing on the sidelines and watching it happen wasn't going to be easy.

An ambulance was parked outside the *clinique* and an inert figure was being stretchered inside, using the entrance at the side of the *porte à tambour* which didn't have any steps. This entrance led straight into the area which served as their emergency department, although in the normal course of events the *clinique* didn't cater for emergency patients.

Alyssa and Pierre followed the stretcher inside, where they found another patient already being treated by Yves Grandet.

The consultant turned to acknowledge Pierre and Alyssa. 'I was at a dinner party with friends in this arrondissement when the call came,' he explained. 'I was able to get here very quickly. Can you get the X-ray department up and running, Pierre?'

'I've just phoned a radiographer. She'll be here in a few minutes, I hope. I'll deal with this man here—Alyssa, could you take that patient into a cubicle and…? Ah, there you are, Sylvie…'

Pierre looked relieved to see his orthopaedic sister arriving.

Alyssa bent over her unconscious patient. He was breathing normally but there was no other sign of life. She placed her stethoscope and listened to his heartbeat. Too slow. She checked out his head. Amid the stubbly dark hair of his crew cut she could discern the development of an ominous bruise. Checking out his limbs and torso, she couldn't find any further signs of injury.

Everything pointed to concussion. She noted the time so that she would know how long he'd been unconscious.

'Il est là!' A petite, smartly dressed Parisian lady came rushing into the department and burst into Alyssa's cubicle. 'Oui, c'est mon mari, Hubert! But he's so still and quiet. Has he been awake since you brought him in?'

'I believe Hubert has been knocked unconscious during the crash,' Alyssa said. 'We're going to admit him to the clinique for tests so that we can ascertain—'

Alyssa broke off as her patient opened his eyes. He stared around him. 'Where am I?'

'You're in the Clinique Ste Catherine,' Alyssa said gently. 'You were involved in a road accident on the Périphérique. The car you were driving was—'

'I wasn't driving a car. My mother says I can learn to

drive as soon as… Is my mother here? Does she know I came home early from school and…?'

'Hubert, what on earth are you talking about?' said his distraught wife. 'I'm here, darling…'

The patient frowned up at the excitable woman. 'Who are you? Don't you dare call me darling! I want to see my parents, not you—whoever you are.'

'I'm your wife!'

Hubert began to laugh in a giggling, childish manner. 'Don't be so stupid. You're much too old to be my wife. I'm only fourteen, so how can I possibly be married?' He looked up at Alyssa with pleading eyes. 'Get this woman away from me. I've never seen her before in my life.'

'I'm Giselle,' the woman cried. 'Look at me, Hubert!'

Hubert turned his head away from his wife as Alyssa put restraining hands on her narrow shoulders.

'I'm afraid this is all part of the concussion, Giselle,' Alyssa explained gently. 'It sometimes happens that concussed patients regress into childhood. Usually not for long. I would hope that we might see some improvement soon, but it's difficult to say how long it will take. If you'd like to give me some details about your husband, I'll admit him to a ward and you can come back in the morning. It's too stressful for him if you remain here while he's feeling unsure of what's happening.'

Giselle became calmer as she listened to Alyssa's words. After a few seconds' hesitation she was able to give Alyssa the details she required about Hubert, both personal and medical. Hubert, it seemed, was a successful lawyer who had been returning home this evening. He'd telephoned his wife to say he would be about an hour late because he was with an important client. Giselle had been entertaining their dinner guests as she'd waited for his delayed arrival.

When the phone call had come from the police, who'd

checked Hubert's wallet and diary, Giselle had left her guests and driven straight to the *clinique*.

'So, shall I go home and come back in the morning, Doctor?' Giselle asked in a tearful voice.

'That would definitely be the best course of action,' Alyssa said soothingly. 'Meanwhile I'll have Hubert checked out by a neurologist and I'll be able to give you a much better prognosis tomorrow.'

Giselle leaned across the stretcher and attempted to kiss her husband, only to be roughly rebuffed by him.

'Get off me, you dreadful woman. Doctor! Take this woman away…'

'Yes, yes, Hubert. Giselle is just going.' Alyssa took hold of Hubert's hand, feeling terribly sorry for the other woman as she left with tears in her eyes.

The patient clung to her hand as if it was a lifeline. 'Can I see my parents now?' he asked in a small voice. 'They'll need to write a note to my teacher if I'm going to stay in hospital. And I want to ask them if I can go on the skiing trip with the school party in February. Will I be better by then?'

'We'll have to see,' Pierre said, coming up behind Alyssa. He lowered his voice. 'I saw you were having problems, Alyssa. I've contacted our consultant neurologist and he'll be in later tonight. We could well find that his memory has returned by the morning, in which case we shall only have to keep him in for observation for a few days.'

'And if his memory doesn't return?' Alyssa asked Pierre.

Pierre frowned. 'Then we've got problems. But we've got a good neurology team who'll do all they can.' He turned to their patient and held a mirror in front of him. 'Would you like someone to comb your hair, Hubert?'

The patient stared into the mirror. 'That's not me; that's my dad!' He stared more closely. 'No, it's not Dad. But it's not me, either. You're trying to play a joke on me. Give me a proper mirror.'

'Hubert, you've lost part of your memory,' Pierre said patiently. 'But hopefully it will return when you get stronger.'

'You took a nasty knock on the head when all the cars smashed into each other,' Alyssa said gently. 'We're going to take you up to the ward now and make you comfortable.'

A nurse took over from Alyssa and walked beside the trolley as a porter pushed it away along the corridor.

'Hubert is actually forty-four years old,' Alyssa told Pierre.

'I know. He's a very distinguished lawyer. His wife must be distraught with worry about him.'

'She is. Let's hope the neurologist can do something to help him…'

'Ah, here comes our consultant. Perhaps you could fill him in on the details of the case, Alyssa, while I deal with another patient?'

In the early hours of the morning the emergency area resembled the aftermath of a battle. Doctors and nurses had tried to cope with the chaotic situation, but it wasn't until the last patient had been discharged or admitted to one of the wards that they were able to restore some kind of order to the department. One by one, the staff left. An exhausted Sylvie said goodnight to Alyssa and Pierre before going away to her room in the medical staff quarters.

Alyssa began to clear the trolley she had used, throwing everything disposable into the nearby bin. She realised that she was working like an automaton, her mind having ceased to function. She and Pierre were the only staff.

'I think you ought to go and get some sleep, Alyssa,' Pierre said, coming up behind her and putting his hands on her shoulders. 'You feel very tense. What you need is a long hot soak in the bath first.'

For a few seconds, under the guise of being a doctor, Pierre was able to massage the tense knots of muscle around Alyssa's shoulderblades.

'Mmm, that feels wonderful,' Alyssa said, instinctively closing her eyes as she leaned back against Pierre's chest.

Whatever am I doing? she thought, without opening her eyes. If she stopped all rational thought just now, she could put the clock back eight years and give herself up to the erotic sensations that were claiming her senses. She could collapse into Pierre's arms and...

'No!'

She was so dead on her feet that she hadn't realised she'd actually spoken out loud. She swung round to look at Pierre and saw the tender expression in his eyes.

'I think you're right about the bath,' she said quickly, in as normal a voice as she could possibly muster under the circumstances. 'Trouble is I've only got a shower, and that's not half as soothing.'

'I've got a wonderful bath—big enough for two.'

Pierre's answer was predictable. Alyssa realised she was boldly holding his gaze but she couldn't help flirting. She was so tired that her brain had simply stopped functioning. How could she be so brazen when she was trying so hard to remain platonic? She felt as if she herself had been in the car crash on the Périphérique and had come out of it with no memory of the last eight years. She and Pierre were still lovers. Any moment now he would carry her off to his apartment, run a hot, scented bath, lift her in, run his tantalising fingers over her skin and...

'It really is time you went off duty.'

Pierre's seductive voice brought her back to the present.

'You'd better forget my offer of a bath for two,' he said gently, reaching out to touch the side of her cheek. 'That really doesn't fit into our lives any more, does it?'

She put up her hand to touch his fingers as they rested on her cheek.

'No, it doesn't,' she said, trying hard to convince herself.

It would be so easy to give in to her natural inclinations. They were the last of the medical staff left. Nobody would see them slipping away down the road if... But they mustn't.

Pierre bent his head and touched her cheek with his lips. *'Bonne nuit, ma petite princesse, dors bien.'*

She hadn't thought Pierre would call her his little princess ever again. It was the name he'd given her when they were lovers. The name he'd always said in their most tender moments. But maybe it had been a slip of the tongue, because he'd already turned from her and was striding purposefully away.

She put her hand to her cheek, on the place where he'd kissed her. It was too poignant a moment to be alone. She wanted to erase the last eight years, to run after Pierre and tell him none of it had happened. They were still young and carefree and...

With a sigh, she forced herself back to reality.

Outside, on the steps of the *clinique*, Pierre paused to take deep breaths of the cold night air. He needed something to calm his emotions. He'd almost given in and confessed that he'd been living only half a life since Alyssa had broken up their relationship.

How long would it take to get her out of his system? At times Alyssa seemed exactly like the young girl he'd known. But then something would happen to change their new rapport and she would be at pains to make it obvious that now, eight years on, she was a totally different woman. An independent woman who didn't want him to interfere in her new life.

He ran down the remaining steps, moving quickly along the deserted street to the door of his prestigious apartment block. An apartment block 'of great standing' was how it had been described in *Le Figaro* when he'd first bought it, ten years ago. He'd rented it out when he went to the West Indies and it had provided a sizeable income for him over the years. It was fortunate that his tenants had been moving out just at the time he'd come back for his three-month holiday.

Some holiday this had turned out to be! He punched in the numbers of the code necessary to open the large front door, crossed the woodblock floor of the foyer and took the thickly carpeted stairs to the second floor two at a time. The lights of the corridor were dimly lit as he made for his oak front door, with its discreet spyhole that helped him to sort out the desired from the undesired visitors when he was on the other side.

Turning the key in the lock, he reminded himself that he would have to be firm with his emotions if he was to survive until Christmas in this strange, unreal relationship with Alyssa. As soon as Dr Cheveny returned from sick leave he could relinquish his post and go back to the West Indies. Once more in the sun, with the surroundings of his established life, it would be easier to forget Alyssa.

But meeting her each day like this, it was far too tempting to believe that she hadn't really changed, that she would open up to his advances and decide that she could compromise on her idea of total independence. Why on earth had she come back? If all she wanted was to be independent, it didn't make sense for her to stir up the past.

He bent down and picked up the letters from the mat, carrying them through into his sitting room. He sank down on to the sofa where he'd so often made love with Alyssa, and suddenly gave a deep sigh. One of the things about coming back here was the wonderful memories of Alyssa that it evoked. Burying his head in the sofa cushions, he tried to conjure up the scent of her body, the feel of her skin against his.

No! He must pull himself together. Quickly he leapt off the sofa and headed for the bathroom. This wouldn't do! Anyway, the apartment needed complete refurbishment. Nearly everything in it was ten years old. Time for a total change. He would just have to accept that Alyssa was a different woman, and that trying to resurrect the past was futile.

As the water from her shower cascaded over Alyssa she closed her eyes and turned her head upwards, feeling the soothing spray on her eyelids. This way she hoped she could blot out all thoughts of Pierre. Because if she didn't, even though she was dead tired, she would find it impossible to sleep.

Just one evening spent with Pierre and her feelings for him had become stronger than they'd ever been. She was eight years more mature now, with a woman's needs and feelings, and at this moment she wanted Pierre so badly she was physically hurting inside.

CHAPTER FOUR

ALYSSA accepted the cup of coffee which Sylvie was holding out towards her. The two of them were taking a mid-morning break whilst reviewing the treatment of their patients.

'Not much we can do about Hubert Legrange,' Sylvie said. 'He's simply refusing to let us move him to the neurology unit.'

Alyssa took a sip of her coffee. 'He told me he likes being in this ward. This was where he was first admitted and I think he feels safe with the people he's got used to.'

Sylvie frowned. 'His wife wanted to have him moved to a private room but he refuses to be parted from Alain, our motorbike crash victim.'

Alyssa smiled. 'Well, Alain is only eighteen, and Hubert, who's still convinced he's fourteen, finds him a good friend.'

Sylvie nodded. 'I'd hoped we would make some progress in three weeks, but Hubert is still in the same state as when he came in.'

Alyssa leaned back against her chair. 'Three weeks! I can't believe I've been working here so long! In one way it feels like only yesterday since I first arrived, and in another it feels like years. We've admitted so many different patients, and I feel I've learned so much since I came here.'

'You've settled in as if you'd been here for years,' Sylvie said, putting the last set of case notes on the pile that had to be returned to the ward. 'The orthopaedic team will be sorry to see you go next week.'

'Next week? I'm not going anywhere, as far as I'm concerned…'

The door of the office opened and Pierre stood in the doorway, as if waiting to be invited into Sylvie's inner sanctum, as everyone called it. Coffee in here was strictly by invitation only. Pierre might be the director of the establishment but he knew his place.

Sylvie's face brightened. 'Do come in, Pierre. Coffee? I was just saying to Alyssa—'

'I didn't know I was moving,' Alyssa said, looking enquiringly at Pierre.

He lowered himself into an armchair next to Sylvie, stretching out his long legs in front of him.

'I was going to discuss it with you, Alyssa, but I've been so busy it simply slipped my mind. I remember when you first came you said you'd be happy to move on to obstetrics when you'd had a spell in orthopaedics. You thrive on versatility, you told me.'

'Yes, but now that I'm settled here I…'

Pierre raised an eyebrow as he looked across at her. 'Settled? I didn't think you were the settling kind.'

Alyssa drew in her breath. Really, Pierre could be so infuriating! During the last three weeks she'd had to cope with her feelings of longing to be alone with him whilst knowing that she mustn't give in. And, not content with simply being around far too much for her emotional stability, Pierre was constantly referring to her desire for independence, her need to move on.

They hadn't repeated the experience of going out together again. The whole of that evening had been far too poignant. On the one hand Alyssa was relieved that Pierre hadn't asked her for another date, but on the other, her perverse side, she longed for another attempt at achieving a platonic friendship. Anything was better than the situation now, of working with Pierre in the *clinique* and wondering how he was spending his off-duty time.

She swallowed hard. 'I'm equally interested in obstetrics and gynaecology,' she said evenly. 'So if that's where I'm required I'll be happy to move on.'

'Splendid!' Pierre said in a relieved tone. 'We'd like you to move to obstetrics in a couple of days.'

'Fine!'

Alyssa deliberately averted her eyes from Pierre. It was the best way of keeping up a professional relationship with him.

'We'll be sorry to see you go, but you'll love it down there,' Sylvie said. 'They have a great time at Christmas on the obstetrics ward. There's such a happy feeling when a new baby is born around Christmas. The patients and staff make a point of having a special celebration.'

'Sounds great!' Alyssa managed to smile, hoping that she would be able to cope with the emotional aspect.

She would have to be totally professional and not allow herself to become sentimental over the new Christmas babies. Her eyes moistened as she thought about the tiny little baby that she and Pierre should have had. Looking across the room, she saw that Pierre was watching her with an anxious expression in his eyes.

'Are you feeling OK, Alyssa?' he asked, gently.

'I'm fine—absolutely fine.'

'You don't look—'

There was a light tapping on the door before a young nurse burst in. 'Sister, Hubert Legrange is creating a terrible fuss. He's dangerously excited and nobody on the ward can calm him down. I'm afraid that he might harm himself.'

The junior nurse hovered uncertainly in the doorway.

'I'm coming!' Sylvie was on her feet, racing out through the door, followed quickly by Pierre and Alyssa.

They found Hubert standing by his bed, shouting down the ward, 'I want my wife! Where's Giselle? Get me out of this place. What am I doing here?'

Pierre took hold of Hubert's arm and began to speak to him in calming tones.

'Please, Hubert, don't make any more fuss. We're all here to help you.'

Hubert looked around him, his expression one of bewilderment, but he took hold of Alyssa's outstretched hand.

'You've been looking after me, Doctor, haven't you?' Hubert said in a quiet voice. 'There's nothing wrong with me, is there? I remember I was driving home on the Périphérique, and…and then it's all blank. I just woke up now, in this bed, and nobody will tell me…'

'Hubert,' Pierre said in a firm but gentle voice, 'you've been here three weeks—since you were involved in a car crash. You were suffering from memory loss and thought you were only fourteen, so—'

'But that's ridiculous! I'm forty-four. How could I…?'

'It sometimes happens,' Pierre said.

'But what about my wife? Has she been in to see me?'

'You didn't know who she was,' Alyssa said carefully. 'So the neurologist who was treating you thought it best she didn't visit you any more. If you'd like to see her now…'

'Well, of course I'd like to see her now!'

'I'll get a message to Madame Legrange immediately,' Sylvie said soothingly.

Hubert leaned forward, towards Sylvie. 'And if you could find me a private room, Sister, I would prefer to be on my own. I need to get back to work as soon as possible. Ask my wife to bring in my laptop, and any paperwork that's accumulated since my accident.'

Pierre assigned a specialist neurology nurse to remain with Hubert until the neurological consultant arrived. As they moved away from Hubert's bed Pierre asked Alyssa if she would come down to his office for a few minutes.

'Of course. What did you want to see me about?'

Pierre smiled. 'Don't look so worried! I simply wanted to explain the new work roster.'

'You mean you thought you should explain why Sylvie knew about my move to obstetrics and gynaecology before I did,' Alyssa said quietly.

Pierre hesitated. 'That does come into it, yes. If you've time to come down now…?'

Alyssa nodded. 'You're the boss.'

Neither of them spoke as they went down in the lift together. The professionalism that was needed cloaked any feelings they might have for each other. Alyssa was utterly scrupulous in observing protocol whenever she found herself working with Pierre. It was the only way she could survive the maelstrom of her emotions.

Once in Pierre's office she sat down at the other side of the desk from him, looking across as she waited for him to elaborate.

Pierre cleared his throat. 'I made the work roster when you first arrived, Alyssa. I assure you that you really did give me the impression that you enjoyed a certain versatility in your work. So I'm sorry if you would have preferred to stay in orthopaedics. Sylvie tells me that she's spoken to the sister in obstetrics and the entire team is looking forward to having you work there.'

'It seems everybody knows about this move except me.'

Pierre ran a hand through his hair. 'Alyssa, there just hasn't been an opportunity to talk to you in the last few days.'

'Yet you found time to talk to Sylvie.'

'We happened to be having dinner together and Sylvie asked me how long you would be working in her department.'

Alyssa could feel a cold hand clutching at her heart.

'And where were you and Sylvie having dinner together?' she asked quietly, hating herself for being so petty but unable to stop the jealous query from escaping her lips.

After a long pause, Pierre finally spoke. 'Well, well. I won't flatter myself by presuming to think you're jealous. But if you'd really like to know we were at the restaurant where I took you before the theatre, three weeks ago. And, yes, before you ask, the fish was superb—as always. But Sylvie doesn't like *escargots* so she had the *pâté maison* instead, which she said was delicious. Anything else you'd like to know about our evening?'

Pierre was trying to glare across the desk at Alyssa, but glaring wasn't something he was any good at. He tried to look fierce and knew he'd failed miserably. How could Alyssa expect him not to hope that she might have feelings of jealousy where other women were concerned?

He sighed. 'Alyssa, Sylvie and I are just good friends, nothing more. I want to make that clear, even if it makes no difference to you.'

Alyssa put a hand to her forehead, resting her elbow on the arm of her chair. She couldn't bear being at loggerheads with Pierre. This situation was all her own fault. She shouldn't have come back here, searching for something that would lay the ghost of her affair with Pierre. When she'd found that the ghost was well and truly alive she should have gone straight back to London. She mustn't meddle in Pierre's life any more. She must allow him to get on with it and not interfere. But still, she couldn't suppress the feeling of relief that he and Sylvie were only friends.

For an instant she closed her eyes, to crystallise what she was going to say. The next thing she knew, Pierre's arm was around her shoulder and he was leaning over her. 'What's the matter?'

'I'm feeling tired, that's all,' she improvised, opening her eyes to look up at Pierre.

Just making eye contact threw her completely. This was the first time she'd looked into his eyes in three weeks, and at such close quarters the experience was turning her legs to jelly. It was a good thing she was sitting down otherwise she might have fallen into his arms.

'It's all such a strain,' she admitted weakly. 'Being here with you, in this same building where…where it all started. Sometimes I think…'

He knelt down beside her, putting comforting arms around her, holding her head against his chest. His jacket had fallen open and she could feel the smooth texture of his silk shirt against her cheek, whilst the distinct scent of his cologne aroused those sensual memories.

'Sometimes you think what, *ma princesse*?' he whispered huskily in her ear.

'Don't, Pierre! Don't call me by that name. You know how—' She broke off as she felt her treacherous body reacting to his closeness.

Gently, he took hold of her hands and pulled her to her feet, so that he could mould his body against hers. She sighed as she felt the beloved contours of his body fitting against hers, as they had done so often before in that fantastic other world of years gone by. This was where she belonged, and she knew nothing could ever change that.

His lips claimed hers and she gave in, lovingly, to his gentle kiss. But a gentle kiss was not enough. She couldn't hold back her longing to be taken completely. This small token of love would always have been the precursor to something more satisfying. Her body needed consummation.

As his kiss deepened she revelled in the frisson of excitement, the liquid desires stirring deep down inside her, the feeling that this was so right for both of them, that they simply had to come together and make love until all their passions were spent…

'No!' She moved suddenly as the feeling of wild abandon threatened to engulf her senses. Looking up into his eyes, she smothered a groan. She wanted Pierre so much, but she mustn't allow herself to be carried away.

'Oh, Pierre,' she said softly, 'what are we going to do?'

He gazed down at her, his eyes, so full of love and longing, mirroring her own.

'You're the one who changed the rules, Alyssa. Are you telling me that you still have feelings for me in spite of…?'

'If you only knew!' she said, her body aching with the frustration and futility of the situation. 'If only—'

She broke off. She'd said too much already.

Pierre dropped his hands to his sides and took a step backwards, leaving a fair distance between them.

'Look, we can't go on like this.' He shook his head in despair.

Alyssa gazed at him, the object of all her affections, and longed to be taken in his arms again. But he was making an effort and so must she.

'Would you like me to leave the *clinique*?' she asked quietly.

He hesitated, before taking a deep breath. 'No, I think we can work this out together. It won't be long before I leave the *clinique* myself, and the problem will be solved anyway.'

He turned away and walked over to the window, staring out over the garden. 'Christmas is on its way, and then…' He turned, forcing himself to smile. 'What we need is some time together that isn't fraught with emotion. Let's go for a walk in the Bois de Boulogne, like we used to do when we had a problem to think through.'

She smiled back, her spirits lifting. 'When did we ever have a problem in those days?'

He took a step towards her, seemed to think better of it and began organising the top of his desk, his eyes intent on the task in hand.

'Oh, we had a few minor hitches, as I recall… Look, go and get out of that ridiculously severe suit and into something that won't spoil if you find yourself rolling amongst the leaves.'

Warning bells began ringing in the sensible part of her mind. 'I hadn't intended to roll in the leaves, Pierre.'

'Joke, Alyssa!' he said in an exasperated tone. 'It was supposed to be a joke. I know your days of rolling around on the ground having fun are well and truly over. You're much too sophisticated for anything so ridiculous.'

She bridled. Was that how he saw her now? A serious, sophisticated career woman? Well, that was the image she'd tried to portray, so she mustn't complain if she'd well and truly succeeded.

'I thought I was supposed to be on duty,' she muttered.

'There's nothing the orthopaedic team can't handle without you,' Pierre said firmly. 'And you need a couple of days off before you start on your new ward. Take the rest of the day off, and that's an order.'

As she turned to move towards the door he looked up from his desk. 'I'll come up and collect you from your room in about an hour. I've got to clear my desk and explain what's happening to my secretary.'

She turned at the door. 'And what *is* happening?' she asked softly, her heart beating so loudly she was sure he would hear it from the other side of the room.

He raised his eyes to hers. 'It's called getting to know you second time around—in a platonic way. We can't go on as we have been during the past three weeks, so it's off with the old and on with the new. And out there in the fresh air, with all those joggers flying past us, we can't get up to any mischief, can we?'

He was grinning at her, that wicked boyish grin that always made her body melt with longing. She yearned to go back into his arms, tell him that she didn't want to form a new relationship. The old one was all she needed.

In her room, Alyssa pulled off the detested suit. She'd thought she looked so smart in it, that it was perfect for her role of doctor in a prestigious *clinique*, but obviously Pierre didn't like the new image she portrayed.

She sat down on the bed for a moment, looking at the crumpled heap of clothes on the floor. Pierre had always preferred her in casual clothes, which were the only kind of clothes she'd possessed when she was last here. So he would approve of the old jeans she was going to put on for their walk in the Bois de Boulogne.

But should she really be seeking Pierre's approval? Did she want him to look at her and admire the way she looked? Wasn't she supposed to be keeping this relationship cool so that neither of them would hurt too much when it finished around Christmas?

She put the probing thoughts to the back of her mind, knowing full well that she wanted Pierre to look at her and admire her in the way he always had during their affair.

She'd always delighted in finding something that made his eyes sparkle with admiration, made his fingers reach for the fabric to check what it was made of. And then, at the end of the day, he would slowly remove the new garment, toss it on the floor and...

This kind of reminiscence would get her nowhere! If Pierre could make the effort to form a new workable relationship, then so could she. After all, it was harder for him. He was the one who thought she'd chosen to break up their affair. She was the only one who knew the truth.

Reaching into the bottom of the wardrobe, she pulled out the old jeans she'd stashed away in a pile of garments that she'd thought she probably wouldn't wear. At the time, when she'd unpacked her suitcase, she'd wondered why on earth she'd brought such a tatty pair of jeans from England. Likewise the white polo neck sweater that she'd mended where it had snagged when she and Pierre were in the woods one time.

But now she remembered quite clearly how she hadn't had the courage to throw out these two items from her wardrobe at home. She'd kept them because they reminded her of her wonderful walks in the Bois de Boulogne with Pierre. And, yes, once they had rolled in the leaves. It had been September, and some of the leaves had started to fall early. They'd been red and gold; she remembered the vivid colours as if it were only yesterday. Pierre had picked up a handful and tried to push them down the neck of her sweater, and they had finished up rolling on the ground, laughing as she made valiant but useless attempts to stop him from behaving like a demented teenager.

So that was why she'd brought these clothes to Paris in her suitcase! Simply to have them here as a dangerously nostalgic reminder of what had happened long, long ago in another life...

Someone was knocking on her door. Please don't let it be Pierre! I'm not ready...

She pulled up the zip on her jeans and struggled into the white sweater, smoothing it down over her tummy.

Running to the spyhole in her door, she looked through. Pierre's brown eyes stared back at her. She unlocked the door, running a hand through her very ruffled hair as she stood back to allow him to enter.

'I hadn't expected you so soon,' she said breathlessly, wishing she hadn't wasted so much time. 'I haven't finished my make-up, and...'

He stood near the door, looking down at her, his eyes full of undisguised admiration. 'I prefer you without make-up. I meant to tell you that before, but I didn't think it fell within my job specification as *médecin-chef* of the *clinique.*'

He looked around him. 'So this is where you live.'

'Small, but cosy, and I'm getting used to living in one room again. Although I have to say I hadn't intended to entertain the boss here.'

Pierre smiled. 'I thought it would be better if we didn't meet in the foyer, where everyone would see us going off for a walk in the middle of the day.'

'A perfectly innocuous walk.'

'Absolutely!'

She drew in her breath. 'Don't look at me like that, Pierre!'

He put his hands on her shoulders, his fingers smoothing over the rough texture of her sweater.

'Like what?' he said with mock innocence. 'I was simply trying to think where I've seen this sweater before, and now I remember.'

She held her breath. 'And where was that?'

'On the floor of my sitting room—and I do believe those are the jeans that went with it.'

'Pierre, don't remind me of—'

She broke off as she looked up into his eyes. It was no good. She couldn't hold out against this powerful feeling of love.

'Don't remind you of what?' he asked huskily.

'Pierre, I'm trying hard to control my feelings, but it's almost impossible. So...' Hesitantly she began to outline the plan that had sprung into her mind. 'I've been wondering if...if this new platonic relationship we're supposed to be having could include some innocuous lovemaking. Do you think we could have a light-hearted affair that will end at Christmas?'

He stared down at her with mock solemnity. 'You mean a sort of hello, goodbye, been nice knowing you sort of affair?'

His fingers tightened on her shoulders. She groaned with the agony of her frustration.

'Yes, yes—but don't make it sound so cold-blooded. I still feel... I'm still very fond of you, and being with you would...'

He lowered his head and covered her quivering lips. She sighed. Another second and she would have wept if Pierre hadn't kissed her. She knew she was being weak by giving in like this, but a light-hearted affair was the only solution that would save her sanity until she and Pierre had to split up again.

As she felt the excitement coursing through her she knew her body was out of control. With a sigh of delicious anticipation she gave herself up to the out-of-this-world experience that she knew would follow.

Pierre's hands were caressing her, gently fingering the restrictive garments. She tugged at her sweater, helping him to remove it. Slowly he unbuttoned the shirt under-neath before reaching for the clasps at the back of her bra. She leaned forward to help him and put her hands on his chest to unbutton his shirt. She could feel the sensual pace quickening. They were both impatient to feel their skin touching, to feel the electric current of passion that had always shot through them at this point.

Gently he carried her over to the bed, shedding garments on the floor as they moved. She moaned with anticipation as he laid her down. As his body covered hers she gave herself up to the thrill of his caresses. His tantalising fin-gers were moving, exploring, turning her body into a fiery furnace of passion where the flames were growing hotter and hotter.

She strove to melt herself into his adored body, to make herself one with him, and when he entered her she gave a gasp of sheer ecstasy at the wonder of their renewed bond-ing. Her passions rose higher and higher as the rhythm of their coupling increased. Feeling him moving inside her, she wanted to weep with joy at this unbelievable union of souls who should never have been parted. And as the ul-timate climax drove her to the heights of sensual delirium she cried out at the wonder of an experience made in heaven...

It was the shrilling of a mobile phone that wakened her. The distinctive sound wasn't her mobile, so whose was it? Then she remembered. Turning her head, she saw that the head on the pillow next to hers was Pierre's. The phone was still ringing, but he ignored it as he brought his lips down on hers.

'Let them leave a message,' he whispered huskily. 'I'm in no state to put on my *médecin-chef* voice and make decisions.'

She revelled in the touch of his lips, the saltiness of his damp skin. She couldn't recall how many times they'd made love. It had been the most momentous reunion of all time!

The phone stopped ringing. Pierre, taking his time, rolled out of the small bed and searched in his trouser pockets for his mobile. He climbed back into bed after checking the message. 'It's only my secretary. She says it's not urgent but she'd like me to call within the next hour. I'll get it over with so that we can go out for that walk we promised ourselves.'

He lay back against the pillow as he phoned his secretary. Alyssa smiled as she heard him saying how delightful it was to be out in the Bois de Boulogne. The trees were a bit bare but…

Alyssa smothered a giggle as Pierre's hand strayed across her breasts whilst he was speaking. He was talking in an efficient, no-nonsense voice that would convince his secretary that everything was under control. He might be taking a few hours off, but he still had his finger on the pulse.

He put the phone down and rolled over to look at her. 'Sidonie wanted to know which surgical consultant she should call in for an operation scheduled for two days' time. The surgical firm can't come to an agreement and I have the casting vote on these occasions. I've given her the names of two suitable consultants that she can contact. Now, where were we…?'

'Don't you think we should go for that walk now?'

Pierre grinned. 'I think you're right. Otherwise we could be here a long time.'

He reached forward and kissed her gently on the lips. 'It's so wonderful to be with you again, Alyssa. I wish we'd thought of this sooner. A light-hearted affair that will finish at Christmas. What a brainwave!'

She swallowed hard as she felt the tears pricking at the back of her eyes. The thought of splitting up from Pierre again was impossibly cruel. She wouldn't think about it while they were together again. She would live for the moment, as she was doing now.

Quickly she pulled herself away and got out of bed. 'Race you to the shower!'

Pierre's long legs overtook her, and he was able to pull her—all the while making mock protestations—into the tiny shower with him. He turned on the wrong tap and cold water cascaded over them, causing her to scream. Laughing, he found the other tap, holding her against his comfortingly warm body, caressing her gently. And then he was rubbing scented foam over her as the water soothed her.

Her nerve-endings were still highly charged, sensitively alive with the excitement of their lovemaking. She was still on cloud nine. Even the cold water that had initially startled her couldn't dampen her high spirits. But at some point she knew she would have to return to earth.

Somehow Alyssa managed to convince herself that a walk in the Bois de Boulogne was a better idea than returning to bed with Pierre. From the vibes she was getting she knew that Pierre thought otherwise, but she wanted to see how their new relationship would hold up when they got outside into the cold afternoon.

It was an unreal situation that they were in. They'd both gone back to the easygoing rapport that had existed between them before. It had been so easy to make love together, so natural, and yet so out of this world. It was as if they'd never been apart, and yet, at the back of her mind, Alyssa had to accept that it was only a temporary situation.

She had to enjoy every stolen moment and then steel herself to say goodbye.

Christmas would be a time of parting.

Pulling on her sweater, she turned to look at Pierre, who was fully clothed and waiting for her already.

'When exactly is Dr Cheveny coming back?' she asked, trying to sound light-hearted and failing miserably.

'He's making good progress and should be back around Christmas. Just before or just after. His cardiac specialist isn't sure when it will be, but apparently François is keen to take up the reins again. At the moment he's convalescing at his house in Provence, but he's due back in Paris next week.'

She swallowed hard. 'It will be good to see him again. I always found him to be very sympathetic—especially so when I had my interview.'

She turned away so that Pierre couldn't see the moistness in her eyes. 'Come on, let's go for that walk.'

As they crossed the little bridge over the old railway line at the top of the street they looked down into the small park beyond. The red and golden leaves had fallen from the trees and, interlaced in the stark brown winter branches, chains of pre-Christmas lights twinkled, giving the impression of glow worms at the height of summer. The façades of the grand houses around the park, where preparations for Christmas were well under way, had shining lights beamed upon them from their well-tended gardens.

A couple of joggers passed them on their way to the paths that criss-crossed the Bois, and it seemed only natural that Pierre should hold her hand. She wondered how the other medical staff would view them if they were to meet anyone they knew. But she found she didn't care what anyone thought, so long as Pierre didn't. He was the one with something to lose. He was the one who had to find himself a suitable wife at some point. Whereas she only had to content herself with a light-hearted affair.

They walked along the path they'd usually taken before, which led to the Lac Supérieur, the larger of the two lakes in the Bois. The afternoon sunshine was quite warm and they sat down on a seat, watching the sparkling of the sun on the water.

Pierre's fingers firmly enclosing hers gave her a false sense of security. If she closed her eyes now she could return to those heady days when their future together had seemed secure. But she knew she must keep reminding herself that this was only temporary. They had three weeks to enjoy their affair, and then…

'When are you planning to go back to the West Indies, Pierre?'

She was trying so hard to sound as if it didn't affect her, but even to her own ears it didn't sound like that.

'I have to be back there at the beginning of the New Year. My post has been covered by a locum for three months. Every couple of years the medical service out there gives me a three-month holiday. I usually spend part of the time in Paris and then travel somewhere.'

'It sounds an idyllic life.'

'It is.' He hesitated, knowing he was pushing his luck. 'You're not tempted to join me?'

She drew in her breath. 'That's your life, Pierre, not mine. I…I must make my own life.'

'I can see you're still hell-bent on being independent,' he said quietly. 'And I can't help admiring you for sticking to your principles. But I wonder how you'll feel as you grow older and—'

'Don't, Pierre! Please leave me to make my own decisions,' she said quickly. 'Tell me, what exactly do you do when you're working in the West Indies?'

'I'm in charge of the medical care of the inhabitants of a group of islands. Ste Cécile is a beautiful French-speaking island, where I run the medical centre. It's the island where I was born. My father was the doctor there before me. When he retired eight years ago I applied for the post and was accepted.'

'Eight years ago,' Alyssa repeated softly. 'So that was when you left the *clinique*.'

Pierre nodded. 'That was after I asked you to marry me, so that you could come with me and share my life. When you went back to England you gave me the impression that as soon as you'd finished your medical training—'

'Pierre, it wasn't as simple as that. Please don't—'

'OK, OK, I'm sorry. I get the message. I don't under-stand what you're trying to do, but I'm sure you've got it all worked out in that complicated head of yours. You seem to be a bit mixed up, and you're sending out some weird signals, but I'll leave you to work out your own future. Even though I can't help worrying about your hap-piness.'

He put an arm round her shoulders in a comforting ges-ture. 'I'd forgotten that we were supposed to be having a light-hearted affair. It's so easy to slip into our old rela-tionship when we're sitting together here on our favourite seat.'

He jumped up decisively, taking hold of her hands and drawing her to her feet. 'Let's walk again. Talking about the past only makes it worse. We've got to live in the present and enjoy it while we can.'

They took a narrow path through the woods, Pierre hur-rying ahead as the remains of the autumn leaves rustled beneath their feet. Alyssa longed for him to turn round and take her in his arms. That was how he would have behaved in yesterday's romance. But she knew that in this new, artificially constructed temporary relationship they mustn't be too demonstrative in public. Besides, they were eight years older and possibly eight years wiser.

When he finally turned to look at her, as they reached the main road that encircled the Bois, he was smiling his assured, confident smile. Alyssa could see that he'd obviously come to terms with their new situation.

'Would you like to come back to the apartment for supper? Something simple, like one of my omelettes?'

Alyssa smiled. 'You must have read my thoughts. I'm absolutely starving.'

He touched the side of her cheek as he looked down at her with a fond expression. 'So am I. It's been an energetic day and we missed lunch, as I recall.'

'I'd forgotten all about lunch,' she said, looking up into Pierre's eyes as she felt the inevitable stirring of excitement at the prospect of a whole evening with him.

'We had better things to think about,' he murmured huskily. 'Come on, it's getting dark.'

'And cold,' Alyssa said, shivering.

Pierre put his arm round her, as she'd hoped he would. Maybe he wasn't too worried about them being seen in a compromising situation after all. Her heart lifted in spite of the fact that she reminded herself once more she was in a temporary situation. There was no harm in enjoying every moment of her time with Pierre.

CHAPTER FIVE

PIERRE'S apartment was just as Alyssa remembered it. Nothing had changed. The sofa and chairs were still comfortably squashy. Slightly shabbier now, but as infinitely inviting as they always had been. She sank down on to the sofa and put her head back on one of the cushions.

'I was afraid you might have changed everything, Pierre.'

He laughed wryly. 'No chance. I hate change. That's why I'm still living on the island where I was born. But I know I'll have to have this place refurbished soon, or I won't be able to get any tenants to rent it when I go back home to Ste Cécile.'

'I don't think you should change anything,' she said quickly. 'Have you got tenants lined up for next year?'

'Not yet. That's when I was planning to have the refurbishment done.'

An embryonic idea was stirring in her mind. 'If the rent isn't too exorbitant I'd love to take it on.'

'You?' Pierre was staring at her with a puzzled expression on his face. 'Why on earth would you want to live here? I thought you were going to move on again when your contract expired with the *clinique* next May.'

'Well, for a start it's more spacious than my room at the *clinique*,' she improvised. 'And I may want to stay on in Paris—extend my contract, if that's possible, or find another position if it's not.'

She knew she mustn't explain that it would mean she could always be in touch with Pierre. Once she'd conquered her jealousy at the thought of him having a relationship that would lead to marriage and a family she could see him from time to time. That way her heart wouldn't break whenever she had to say goodbye. Having renewed their love again, she knew goodbyes would be agony.

'Well, if you're sure you'd like to rent it we'll come to some amicable arrangement,' he said slowly.

'Why don't I take it on for six months from January?' she suggested. 'That will see me through to the end of my contract with a little time at the end to sort out what I'm going to do next. I can let you know in the spring what my plans are.'

By the spring she hoped she would have made up her mind what she was going to do with the rest of her life. Starting an affair with Pierre again was going to be a life-shattering experience. She no longer knew what she wanted from life, nor where she wanted to go. For the moment she would simply coast, get through one day at a time until it was time to say goodbye. Maybe then her rational thoughts would crystallise, but for the moment all she wanted was to be with Pierre, to love him and be loved by him until the time came for him to go back to the West Indies.

'OK, that's a deal,' he said, his expression still curious. 'But if you change your mind…'

'I won't.'

'It has been known,' he said evenly.

She swallowed hard. 'Yes, but in matters of…er…business I'm always scrupulously correct.'

'Glad to hear it. So, do you think you could whisk up some scrupulously correct eggs while I nip out for some salad and fresh bread? It's after five o'clock so the *boulangerie* will have freshly baked baguettes.'

'Mmm, yummy! Hurry back! I'm starving.'

*   *   *

Alone in Pierre's kitchen, Alyssa found herself singing quietly to herself as she whisked up the eggs.

'''*Il y avait les gros crocodiles et les orangoutans…*'''

She smiled to herself as she realised it was years since she'd sung the little song she'd learned at the kids' club on a beach in Normandy where her grandmother had rented a holiday house one summer. She must be feeling happy and carefree again.

Looking around her, she felt a warm glow deep down inside at the realisation that this was going to be *her* kitchen soon. She would be able to close the doors on her own little kingdom, curl up on the sofa with a good book and feel that in some indefinable way Pierre was still part of her life.

'I'm back!'

Her heart lifted at the sound of Pierre's voice from the tiny hallway. She could hear him kicking off his shoes, putting his jacket in the hall wardrobe, padding over the soft carpet and then into the kitchen. He tossed a fresh baguette along with packets of lettuce, tomatoes, garlic and fresh herbs on to the wooden table.

'You look as if you've moved in already,' he said, coming up behind her and placing his arms around her waist.

She turned in his arms and standing on tiptoe lifted her face to his. Slowly he brought his lips down on hers. She savoured the kiss before gently pulling herself away.

'Your eggs are ready for the difficult omelette operation, sir. I've separated the yolks from the whites so you can do your fantastic soufflé omelette—which I remember used to be the *specialité de la maison* here in this kitchen. Is there anything else you would like me to do? Do you require a scalpel, scissors, local anaesthetic…?'

'You could wash the salad and then sit beside me on this stool and look beautiful.'

She laughed as she picked up the lettuce and walked over to the sink. 'I don't feel very beautiful in this old sweater.'

'You look radiant to me,' he said gently.

She knew that her radiance was something coming from within. She hadn't felt like this when she'd wakened this morning. But after spending most of the day with Pierre there had been a definite transformation.

They sat down at the wooden table when their meal was ready. Pierre sat at the head of the little table, Alyssa on his right side—just as they always had done.

The omelettes were delicious. Putting down her fork at the end of the meal, Alyssa reached across and took hold of Pierre's hand.

'The best omelette I've had in years.'

Pierre looked down at Alyssa's small fingers encircling his own. 'Haven't cooked an omelette like that for years.' He raised his eyes to hers. 'I've always stuck to the plain variety.'

The electric current throbbing between them as their eyes met was too poignant to bear. Looking at Pierre now, Alyssa could see he had that little boy lost look that always melted her heart. What was she doing, denying them both a future together? Why did their situation have to be so complicated?

She stood up and cupped his chin in her hands as she leaned forward to kiss him gently on the lips. 'I'm unsure about everything,' she said sadly. 'But I'm glad we're together again for this brief time.'

He stood up and took her in his arms. 'It doesn't have to be brief. We could—'

Gently she put her finger against his lips. 'Trust me. It's for the best,' she whispered.

'Then let's make the most of every minute,' he said, his voice husky with passion.

She sighed with joyous anticipation as Pierre scooped her up into his arms and carried her through to his bedroom. Gently he laid her on his bed. This time their lovemaking was slow and unhurried—the lovemaking of a couple who'd satisfied every fibre of their physical being earlier in the day but still wanted to reaffirm their love for each other.

She leaned back against the pillows, running her hands over his strong, muscular, athletic body as his caresses started to drive her wild. This night would be their eternity. She would pretend there was no ending to this blissful encounter…

Alyssa awoke with a start and reached out to silence the phone before realising that she wasn't in her own bed. Her body tingled with the aftermath of their lovemaking. She had never experienced such magical passion with Pierre before.

Still remaining in her relaxed euphoric state, she felt a pang of dismay when she heard Pierre telling whoever it was on the phone that he would be at the *clinique* as quickly as possible. Yes, he would meet them there.

She rolled on her side. 'Who was that?'

'Henri Fontaine's wife. You remember Henri? The *clinique* gardener with the shattered leg?'

'Of course. He went home about two weeks ago. What's the problem?'

Pierre was already out of bed, pulling on his trousers, buttoning up his shirt and reaching for his jacket.

'Henri's wife says he's running a high temperature. She

didn't know who to call at the *clinique* so she rang me here. I've told her to bring him back to the *clinique* immediately.'

Alyssa leapt out of bed and reached for her clothes. 'I'll come with you. Sounds as if there could be some infection—either in the bone or the surrounding tissues.'

'Let's hope not. But whatever it is, we must deal with it quickly.'

The lights of the *clinique* were dimmed as Alyssa and Pierre made their way in through the side entrance that led to their small emergency area. Alyssa prepared a patient trolley as they waited for Henri and his wife to arrive. As their car pulled up in front of the *clinique*, they hurried outside.

Madame Fontaine was distraught with worry.

'When I realised how high Henri's temperature was tonight, I knew I couldn't ignore his fever any longer.'

'How long has Henri had a high temperature?' Alyssa asked, as she helped Pierre to manoeuvre the trolley into the treatment area.

'About five days. I thought it was a cold coming on, or a touch of *la grippe*.'

Alyssa nodded. *La grippe*—or flu, as it was called in England—was common in Paris during the winter, and did cause a high temperature, so she could understand Madame Fontaine coming to that conclusion. But with Henri's history of a recent orthopaedic operation it might not be the correct diagnosis.

She looked down at Henri, lying so uncharacteristically still with a worried expression on his face. 'Don't worry, Henri. We'll soon find out what's the matter with you and—'

'It's my leg, isn't it?' Henri said plaintively. 'It's got

nothing to do with *la grippe*. I told Marcelle to bring me back to the *clinique* two days ago, but…'

'Well, you're here now, Henri,' Pierre said quickly. 'Now, I'm just going to open up the window in your plaster to take a look at what's happening.'

Alyssa leaned across their patient as Pierre removed the section of plaster which had been left as an observation window. She could immediately see that there was inflammation and redness around the post-operative wound, which was a clear indication that there was internal infection.

She looked across at Pierre, waiting for him to explain the situation to Henri.

'I'm going to remove your plaster entirely, Henri,' he said carefully. 'We need to see exactly what's going on, but it looks as if there is some infection in your leg. I'm going to put you on intravenous antibiotics and call in Monsieur Grandet—the surgeon who performed your operation.'

'Whatever you say, Doctor,' Henri said in a resigned tone.

'I'll fix a canula in Henri's arm for the antibiotics,' Alyssa said. She turned to look at Henri's wife, who was once more voicing her worried concern about her husband. 'Would you like to take a rest in the little sitting room at the top of the steps, *madame*?'

Madame Fontaine agreed that she would, seemingly relieved to let Alyssa and Pierre take over from her. She'd obviously had a worrying time since Henri fell from his ladder. Pierre had told Alyssa that the *clinique* was continuing to pay Henri's wages, but with the serious state of his leg his wife must have been wondering if her husband would ever be able to continue in his physically demanding job. Coupled with her concern for Henri's health, she had a heavy load on her shoulders.

After Pierre had removed the plaster Alyssa examined the site of the wound. It was badly infected. Pierre drew her to one side to discuss the situation.

'When Yves arrives I think he'll want to take Henri to Theatre,' Pierre said. 'The night staff will provide me with a couple of theatre nurses. I'll arrange for an anaesthetist to come in. In view of your past experience of orthopaedic surgery, would you be willing to assist Yves?'

Alyssa nodded. 'Of course. I'm thinking it could be the steel plates holding the bones in place that are the source of infection. It sometimes happens in patients who've had a complicated fracture—especially if the fractured bones were exposed through the skin at the time of the accident. If there is some infection, it will gravitate and stay around the steel plates. Some patients tolerate internal plating better than others. My guess is that Monsieur Grandet will take out the plates and put external steel rods through the bones to hold them in position.'

'That seems a very good solution to me,' Yves Grandet said, coming in through the door and overhearing what Alyssa was saying.

'*Bonsoir*, Yves,' Pierre said. 'Yes, I think Alyssa will prove to be a good orthopaedic assistant for you.'

'I'm sure she will.'

'I'll be on hand to help if there are problems with closing up the skin,' Pierre told Yves. 'The infection has eroded the area around the initial wound, and some skin grafting may be necessary to help the healing process.'

Yves nodded. 'I remember you specialised in plastic surgery at one point in your career, didn't you? That could be useful to me.'

Alyssa looked up at Pierre questioningly. 'I didn't know you'd worked in plastic surgery.'

'There are a lot of things you don't know about me,' Pierre said quietly. 'I worked in a specialist burns hospital just outside Paris soon after I qualified.'

'You would have made a very fine plastic surgeon,' Yves said, as he leaned over their patient to take a better look at the injured leg. 'But I remember talking to Claude, your father, when he came back to Paris one time. He told me you had this dream of living in the sun on the island where you were born, surrounded by your own large family. He was looking forward to all those grandchildren. Can't think why you're still a bachelor, my boy.'

Alyssa glanced at Pierre and was relieved that he remained silent, his expression giving nothing away.

As the genial orthopaedic consultant examined Henri's leg his expression swiftly changed to concern. Quickly he outlined what he was going to do in Theatre, giving his patient as much information as he thought he would understand.

'So I'm going to Theatre now, am I?' Henri asked in surprise.

Yves nodded. 'The sooner I take a look and find out why your leg is infected the better.' He turned to Pierre. 'How long before the theatre will be ready?'

'It's ready now. And I've almost completed organising the theatre team. As I said, Alyssa will assist you. She's had wide experience of orthopaedic surgery and—'

'Oh, I know all about Alyssa's credentials,' Yves interrupted. 'I checked her out when she first arrived here and went to work with the orthopaedic team. I have to say I've been impressed with her work. She's a very good doctor. Now she'll have to prove to me she's a good orthopaedic surgeon.'

'But you'll be doing the operation, *m'sieur*, won't you?' Alyssa said quickly.

Yves Grandet smiled benignly. 'Of course. But I'll need your expert help.'

With the rest of the theatre team gathered around the operating table, fully gowned and masked, Alyssa waited for Yves to begin the operation. She watched as he carefully opened up the wound from the previous operation. Inside the tissues were inflamed, but the bones appeared to be healthy.

Alyssa leaned forward and took a swab from the infected tissue before placing it in a sterile test tube. Handing it to a nurse, she instructed her on how to label it so that it could be taken to the path lab for histology. Once they had discovered which specific organism was causing the infection they could deal more easily with an antibiotic cure.

Holding back the surrounding tissues with sterile retractors, Alyssa ensured that the orthopaedic consultant had a clear view of the infected area.

'You were quite right, Alyssa,' Yves muttered. 'The infection is all centred around the plates. I'm going to take them out and—'

He broke off, glancing towards Pierre who, also fully gowned and masked, was awaiting further instructions. 'Have you got the steel fixators I asked for, Pierre?'

'They've just arrived,' he said, handing the sterile steel rods to Alyssa.

Yves proceeded to discard the infected plates, before taking the rods from Alyssa and screwing them through the bones to hold them in place. When four fixators had been screwed through the tibia—the main bone running down the front of the leg—and the calcaneum—the heel bone—Yves stood back for a moment to review the situation.

'What do you think, Alyssa?' he said, peering at her over the top of his mask. 'Will that hold the bones in place, do you think?'

He was one of the few men who were barely any taller than she was, and Alyssa felt very comfortable looking eye to eye with this eminent surgeon and giving him her opinion.

'I think the fixators will hold the bones. But there isn't a very good blood supply in that area. Henri's legs are particularly thin around the ankle, so I was wondering if we should do a flap.'

Yves nodded approvingly. 'That's what I was thinking, Alyssa. You've obviously worked on this problem before. Yes, if I turn back a flap of flesh to cover the affected area we'll get a better blood supply to aid the healing process.'

'But turning back a flap will mean that a sizeable area of the leg is exposed without skin, so...' Alyssa looked across at Pierre. 'That's where we'll need your help, Pierre. Can you find a suitable donor site from which to transpose the necessary skin?'

Pierre nodded. 'Yes, I know exactly what I'll do.'

'Don't know why I bothered to come in,' Yves said, with the hint of a chuckle in his voice. 'The two of you could have managed very well without me.'

Yves turned to look at Pierre and Alyssa could see that the eyes above the surgeon's mask were smiling. 'So, where do you propose to transpose this skin from, Pierre?'

'Top of Henri's left thigh...just here,' Pierre said, leaning forward to prepare the donor site. 'Good healthy skin like this is going to serve the purpose.'

Pierre scraped small slivers of skin from the surface epithelium of Henri's thigh, leaving the lower layers of the skin intact, before transferring the tiny slivers to the exposed skinless area of the lower leg. Then he fixed a string of special gentamycin beads near the surface of this area of tissue.

The junior theatre nurse, who hadn't seen gentamycin beads used before, asked Alyssa to explain their purpose.

'Gentamycin beads give antibiotic cover inside the leg for three to four weeks,' Alyssa told the nurse. 'So in about a month, when they've served their purpose, we'll remove them.'

'Does that mean Henri will have to have another operation?' the nurse asked.

'Just a minor operation under local anaesthetic,' Alyssa explained.

As Alyssa finished sewing up the wound at the end of the operation she was careful to leave one of the gentamycin beads outside the wound, to indicate where they were. After this, she stood back to take a critical look at Henri's leg. Pierre moved forward to inspect the finished results more closely.

'Well done, Yves!' Pierre said, before looking down at Alyssa. 'And well done to your surgical assistant.'

Watching Pierre now, Alyssa could see that his eyes were full of admiration.

'Thank you, *m'sieur*,' she said demurely.

'Henri can go to the orthopaedic ward as soon as he comes round,' Yves said, pulling off his gloves and throwing them in the general direction of one of the bins. 'Will you be able to stay on, Alyssa? The first few hours will be critical, and I need a good orthopaedic doctor to be on hand.'

'Of course,' she said. 'I'd like to make sure that nothing goes wrong.'

Yves nodded approvingly. *'Bon!'* He glanced at Pierre.

'Not only beautiful, but talented as well. What a find! I hope you're going to extend Alyssa's contract at the *clinique* for a long time, Pierre.'

'Actually, Yves, it won't be up to me,' Pierre said quietly. 'François Cheveny will be returning around Christmas to take over again.'

'Ah! Well, you must give Alyssa a good report when you speak to François. How is he, by the way? I heard…'

The two men were deep in conversation as they left the theatre, and Alyssa was glad that neither of them had asked her whether she *wanted* to extend her contract. For the moment she wasn't going to think any further than next June. She was going to make the most of her few weeks with Pierre, then she would work through the New Year and the spring, enjoying the fact that she was living in Pierre's apartment.

Earlier in the evening, the idea of staying on as long as she could at the *clinique* and in Pierre's apartment had seemed appealing. But now she wasn't so sure she could handle the emotional turbulence she would experience when Pierre finally found himself a wife. Remaining emotionally detached from a situation like that would be well-nigh impossible.

Better to finish her contract at the end of May, stay on for a couple of weeks to get the apartment ready for the next tenant and then move on. But where she would move to was utterly uncertain. Being with Pierre was proving to be an earth-shattering experience that was causing emotional and mental turbulence. Her future plans were becoming more and more complicated and uncertain…

Someone had put a hand on her shoulder. Alyssa opened her eyes and found a junior nurse smiling down at her.

'You fell asleep, Doctor. Would you like *un petit café noir*?'

Alyssa smiled back, accepting the tiny coffee cup that the nurse was holding out to her. The lights in the orthopaedic ward were being switched on as the nurses began their morning routine. She took a sip of the coffee before placing the cup on her patient's bedside locker. Standing up, she began to readjust the flow of Henri's intravenous drip.

Her patient opened his eyes. 'You still here, Dr Alyssa? I thought you'd have gone to your bed by now. Have you been here all night?'

'Yes, I have, Henri.' She leaned over to examine Henri's leg. Carefully, she adjusted the tube which was draining the infected area. She'd fixed the leg on a rigid plaster back slab to keep it immobile after the operation.

'What are those spikes sticking out of my leg?'

'Those are holding the bones in position, Henri. We had to take out the steel plates because they were acting as a source of infection. That was why you were getting such a high temperature. Your temperature is almost normal again this morning, thanks to the antibiotics.'

'Thanks for all you're doing for me, Doctor.' Henri looked up as Pierre arrived at the bedside. 'I was just saying to Dr Alyssa, it's time she went to bed.'

'That's precisely what I was going to tell her, Henri,' Pierre said.

Alyssa turned and smiled at Pierre. 'I'm OK. Once I've handed over to the orthopaedic team I'll get some sleep. I actually fell asleep in the chair for a little while.'

'I'm not surprised. I'll stay with Henri until Sylvie comes on duty,' Pierre said firmly. 'Take the rest of the day off, and tomorrow as well. Like I said, you need a break before you start work in obstetrics.'

'Alyssa isn't leaving us, is she?' Henri asked anxiously.

Alyssa smiled down at her patient. 'I'm afraid so. But I'll keep popping in to see how you're getting on, Henri.'

'I hope you will,' Henri told her.

Pierre waited until Alyssa had said her goodbyes to the patients she'd worked with most recently. She had to promise all of them that she would return to visit them from time to time. As she made for the swing doors that led away from the main ward, Pierre caught up with her.

'May I see you this evening?' he murmured.

She smiled. 'What did you have in mind?'

'I'll try to get tickets for one of the pre-Christmas concerts at the Ste Chappelle. A small choir and orchestra are doing a series of concerts performing baroque music with a Christmas theme.'

'Sounds interesting.'

'And afterwards I thought we could walk along the Seine, find a little restaurant somewhere and…'

'You just talked me into it,' she said, hoping that she would be able to sleep for a few hours now that she was livening up again. She didn't want to be tired this evening. There weren't many more evenings with Pierre left.

As Alyssa walked into the obstetrics and gynaecology unit she was greeted by the sister in charge. Jacqueline Montigny, a tall, imposing woman in her early fifties, hurried down the ward towards her.

'Ah, Alyssa. How nice to see you again,' the sister said.

Alyssa smiled as she shook the outstretched hand. She'd been introduced to Jacqueline soon after she'd arrived at the *clinique* and found the sister to be friendly and helpful.

'Welcome to obstetrics. According to Pierre, you've had a lot of experience in obstetrics and gynaecology, so I'm sure you're going to be a valuable member of our team.

A new patient has just arrived and I'd be grateful if you could give me some help. Her name is Marie Lefevre.'

Alyssa walked back down the ward with Jacqueline, who paused in front of the bed of a young woman who was sobbing quietly, her hands clutching the sheet that covered her.

'The doctor is here to see you now, Marie,' Jacqueline said, handing a case history file to Alyssa. 'There's very little information in here yet, Doctor, so I'll leave you to it…'

Alyssa bent over her patient and took hold of her hand. 'Now, tell me all about yourself, Marie.'

Marie stifled her sobs. 'I've got this awful pain, Doctor—down here.'

Alyssa pulled the curtains round her patient and turned back the covers on the bed. Marie was indicating the lower right side of her body. Alyssa placed her fingers gently on the affected area and her patient winced.

'I haven't had a period for three months, Doctor, and I know I'm pregnant, although I haven't checked with my doctor. I haven't even told my husband yet, because I've already had two miscarriages and I was waiting until this pregnancy was more established before I told him. Charles is just longing for me to have a baby and I don't want to disappoint him again.'

Alyssa, palpating the abdomen, could feel the tense muscles guarding the tender area. Her awful suspicions were being confirmed and it was all too close to home for her. She was trying to be professional, but flashes of memory kept on reminding her of the devastating time when she herself had been rushed into hospital suffering from an ectopic pregnancy.

'I'm going to examine you, Marie,' Alyssa said in a calm, professional tone.

As she turned to take a pair of sterile gloves from the trolley which a staff nurse had wheeled in, she steeled herself against any emotional involvement. She owed it to this poor, suffering patient to give her all the help and expert care that she needed.

Gently she examined inside the patient's vagina. It wasn't necessary to examine too far because the tell tale signs were there. A brownish discharge—usually referred to as the prune juice discharge—pointed to the obvious diagnosis. Further examination revealed extreme tenderness over the affected Fallopian tube, where Alyssa suspected a tiny embryo had implanted itself instead of into the wall of the womb.

Alyssa peeled off the sterile gloves and glanced at the temperature reading which the staff nurse had produced. She swallowed hard. All the cardinal signs of an ectopic pregnancy were there in front of her. A much-wanted baby was about to terminate its struggle for survival. It held no chance as it grew in the Fallopian tube, and if they didn't get this patient into Theatre and remove the affected tube as soon as possible the tube would rupture with dangerous consequences. The mother's life was at stake as well.

'We're going to take you to the operating theatre, Marie,' Alyssa said gently.

'There's nothing wrong with the baby, is there? I only went to the doctor this morning because I had a pain down here. As I said, I hadn't even told the doctor I thought I was pregnant and… Oh, say I'm not going to lose this one, Doctor. Go on—say it…'

Jacqueline came hurrying through the curtains. 'There, there, Marie. What on earth is the matter?'

The sister glanced at Alyssa's ashen face. 'Are you all right, Doctor?'

'Yes, I'm fine, Sister,' Alyssa said briskly. She lowered

her voice. 'I've examined Marie and I think we should take her to Theatre for an immediate laparoscopy. If, as I suspect, this reveals a tubal pregnancy we'll need a laparotomy to ligate bleeding points and remove the tube.'

'I'll phone Theatre now,' Jacqueline said quickly. 'Staff Nurse will prepare the patient and—'

'Minimum preparation,' Alyssa instructed. 'The main thing is for Marie to be operated on as quickly as possible. She may need a blood transfusion, so I'm going to take a blood sample for grouping and cross-matching, and then I'll set up an intravenous saline drip.'

Jacqueline nodded in agreement before hurrying away.

'I'm going to lose the baby, aren't I, Doctor?' Marie said, her voice shaky but quiet and resigned now.

Alyssa straightened up from taking the blood sample, her heart full of compassion for the ordeal her patient was going through. And she knew, from her own traumatic experience, that the agony had barely started. When the full realisation that this much-wanted baby wasn't going to make it set in...

Alyssa cleared her throat. 'We're doing all we can, Marie. I can't predict how things will go in Theatre, but you're in good hands. I'll make a point of being here when you get back.'

Marie reached out and took hold of Alyssa's hand, squeezing it tightly as the tears ran down her cheeks.

'Make sure you're here, Doctor. You seem to know what I'm going through.'

Alyssa reached for a tissue, dabbing at the moist patches beneath her patient's eyes. She was being most unprofessional, she knew, but even though she was a doctor she was only human. She was beginning to find it impossibly difficult to cope with a situation that provoked so many unhappy memories.

'I'll be here, Marie,' she told her patient, in a calm voice which belied the traumatic turmoil of her emotions.

'So, how did your first day in obstetrics go?' Pierre asked as they sat in a little bar overlooking the Seine. 'You've been unusually quiet all evening. I'm beginning to get the impression you're not happy about something.'

Alyssa took a sip of her wine. The concert they'd attended should have been an uplifting occasion, but she'd found it difficult to concentrate on the music.

There had been no tickets available for the concert in the Ste Chappelle two days ago, so Pierre had bought tickets for this evening, and Alyssa had been looking forward to hearing the prestigious choir and orchestra performing Christmas music. But caring for her ectopic patient, seeing her go through the agonies that she herself had gone through, had been so traumatic that she felt unable to switch off and relax.

Explaining to Marie the implications of the surgical removal of her Fallopian tube when she'd come back to the ward after the operation had left Alyssa feeling drained and emotionally exhausted.

'I'm perfectly happy with the obstetrics unit,' Alyssa said with false brightness. 'I'm a bit tired, that's all. But the concert was so wonderful tonight—it helped to raise my spirits again. I thought the Bach was superb, and listening to it in such a beautiful setting made the music seem to soar up to the high ceiling and pour out through those exquisite stained glass windows...'

'Alyssa, you're not a music critic, preparing your piece for the culture page in *Le Figaro*,' Pierre said gently.

He reached across the table and covered her hand with his own as he interrupted her eulogy. 'You don't fool me one bit. Tell me why you don't like working in obstetrics and then we'll go on to discuss the concert. Until I know what's troubling you I—'

'There's nothing wrong. I do like working in obstetrics. I really do.' Alyssa swallowed hard, hesitating before she continued, 'I got a bit upset about one of the patients who was having a hard time, that's all.'

'You mustn't let yourself become too involved,' he said gently. 'Who was this patient?'

'Oh…a patient called Marie Lefevre. She…she was suffering from an ectopic pregnancy. The foetus was growing in her Fallopian tube, so I arranged for her to be taken down to Theatre and—'

Alyssa could hear her own voice breaking up. She couldn't go on in front of Pierre. It was all too reminiscent of her own traumatic experience eight years ago.

'Go on, take your time, Alyssa.' Pierre's eyes were both sympathetic and questioning. 'I've read the report on Marie, but I can't see why it should affect you like this. Yes, ectopic pregnancies are always traumatic. But you must have experienced numerous ectopic pregnancies during your career. I would have thought—'

'I need some fresh air.' Alyssa stood up. 'It's too stuffy in here. Let's go outside.'

She hurried outside, walking across the cobbled road to lean against the wall that flanked the footpath at the side of the river. Staring out across the deep swirling waters of the Seine, she tried to dispel the images of her own trauma when she'd come round from the anaesthetic to be told she'd lost the baby, had the affected tube removed and, because of complications, would be unlikely ever to conceive again.

She didn't turn as she heard Pierre's footsteps behind her. His arm encircling her shoulders gave her comfort, but she still felt terribly alone in an impossible situation.

'Let's walk along the river path, Pierre.' She moved away from the warmth of his arm.

He took her hand in his, holding it firmly as they walked side by side. She glanced up at the pale December moon. There had been a moon like this peeping through the hospital window on that fateful night when she'd lost their baby.

Suddenly Alyssa knew she couldn't go on alone. This was a problem she had to share with Pierre. Whatever the outcome, she couldn't continue to shoulder this awful burden.

She stopped walking and turned to look up at Pierre. 'You said you thought I must have experienced ectopic pregnancies before and coped with them... Well, yes, I have. Quite a few, in fact. One in particular was...'

'Go on, Alyssa,' he said gently, putting his hands on either side of her shoulders and drawing her towards him.

'I experienced...I went through an ectopic pregnancy myself,' she said, trying to put herself on automatic pilot so that she could continue without breaking down. She didn't know why she was telling Pierre now. It would only make matters worse. But she needed to confide in him, to unburden herself of the secret she'd kept from him so long.

She looked up at the moon again, seeking some kind of inspiration as to how she could best get all this off her chest without hurting Pierre too much.

'There was a December moon just like this on the night I lost my baby,' she said, her voice quivering with emotion.

Pierre's expression was agonisingly tender as he looked down at her, his hands tightening on her shoulders before he moved round to encircle her in his arms.

'A December moon? How long ago was this, Alyssa?'

For a few seconds she remained silent. But she knew

she must go on and tell Pierre everything. She'd got this far. She had to finish what she was going to say to him.

One of the long Parisian *bateaux mouche* was slowly gliding past them. Alyssa looked at the bright lights fixed to the sides of the boat, twinkling out across the water, and realised that this was the moment when everything would change between her and Pierre. But she couldn't find the right words. She remained rooted to the spot, staring at the illuminated interior of the boat which was decorated in a Christmassy fashion for the happy diners who were sampling a Christmas menu.

'The ward was decorated ready for Christmas when I came back from Theatre, Pierre,' she said quietly. 'I remember looking up at a paper streamer above my head. One of the nurses had fixed it there, specially for me. I think it was meant to cheer me up, but…'

She couldn't go on.

Pierre held her so close now that she could feel the pounding of his heart.

'When was this, Alyssa?' he said softly.

'It was…it was eight years ago.'

Pierre released his grip and took a step backwards, staring down at her, his eyes registering bewilderment and disbelief.

'You were pregnant with our child and you didn't tell me?'

'I'd only just found out. I hadn't missed a period,' she said quickly, her thoughts gathering momentum now that she'd made the initial revelation. 'As we both know, that sometimes happens when the pregnancy occurs outside the uterus.'

She mustn't stop now. She could see the sadness in Pierre's expression, but she had to continue.

'I'd done a pregnancy test only the day before, because

I'd been experiencing nausea for a few weeks and my abdomen was beginning to feel tight and swollen. When the test turned out to be positive I phoned you, but all I got was your answering service. I didn't want to leave a message for you to call back because I was on duty for the rest of the day, and I didn't want to have to tell you in front of… Anyway, there was an emergency just as I was going off duty, and by the time I was free it was the middle of the night.'

'You could have wakened me,' Pierre said plaintively. 'With wonderful news like that I—'

'Don't, Pierre! Yes, it was wonderful news. And I thought I had plenty of time to tell you. But in the early hours of the next morning a searing pain in the area of my left Fallopian tube woke me up. I could feel the tense muscles over my abdomen and I knew…I just knew that I was going to lose our baby…'

'*Oh, ma petite princesse,*' Pierre whispered, gathering her back in his arms again. 'Why didn't you call me? I would have come straight over to be with you in hospital. You shouldn't have been alone. It was my baby as well as yours…'

'I knew how sad you would be if I did lose it, and I was hoping that the doctors would say there hadn't been too much damage. If they'd given me a healthy prognosis I would have called you after they removed the affected Fallopian tube and…and the tiny embryo inside. But…but the obstetrics consultant came to see me soon after I came round from the anaesthetic. He told me it had been a difficult operation which had left me with scar tissue and adhesions. He said it was unlikely that I would ever get pregnant again.'

'But that was straight after the operation, Alyssa!' Pierre

cupped her face in his hands, gazing down at her with an anguished expression. 'You would have healed and—'

'No, no.' Alyssa shook her head.

'I was married for four years. Mike had said he didn't want children when I told him I was unlikely to conceive, and at the beginning of our marriage he was relieved about that. After two years Mike changed his mind. Until that time I'd been taking the Pill, because Mike was so dead against starting a family and insisted I take it just in case. When he had this change of heart I stopped taking it. After two years I still wasn't pregnant. That was when Mike told me he was having an affair with Rachel, one of our friends. She was pregnant, so he decided to leave me and move in with her.'

'Sounds like you were well rid of him. But I can't understand why you haven't told me all this before.'

She looked up into his eyes and couldn't bear to see the anxious, hurt expression.

'It's because I love you, Pierre,' she said brokenly. 'I want you to move on and be happy with someone who can give you the family you want. Someone who—'

'But I don't want anyone else. I want you!'

CHAPTER SIX

ALYSSA stared at Pierre, deeply moved by his passionate outburst. She hadn't expected him to believe so positively that a childless relationship between them would be enough for him.

'Yes, I can believe, at this moment, that you think our relationship is worth more to you than having a family,' she said slowly.

'But it is! It's all that matters to me.' Pierre drew her closer in his arms, bending down so that his face was nestling against her hair.

By the pale light of the moon and the overhead lights from the riverside road, Alyssa could see a young couple walking hand in hand towards them. She could feel the trembling of Pierre's body against her own. This wasn't the place to discuss life-shattering problems.

Gently she released herself from Pierre's arms. 'Take me home, Pierre.'

He held her at arm's length, looking down at her with a wistful expression. 'Home? Where's home?'

She gave him a sad smile. 'That was a slip of the tongue. I think I meant your apartment…soon to be my apartment…for a little while. That's where I feel most at home.'

Pierre drew her to him. 'We'll go up to the embankment and get a taxi.'

Alyssa curled her bare feet underneath her on the sofa, reaching up to take the glass of cognac that Pierre was holding out towards her.

'Sip that slowly, until you feel warmer and stronger,' Pierre said. 'It's purely medicinal—I usually find it works on patients who're suffering from shock.'

Alyssa studied Pierre's solemn expression. 'Yes, Doctor. But I thought you were the one who'd had the shock.'

He sat down beside her, cradling his own brandy glass with both hands. 'I've had a tremendous shock. But the full effect of *your* suffering has been delayed for eight years. I could tell you were reliving your traumatic experience down there on the footpath beside the river.'

Alyssa took a sip of her cognac, feeling strength flowing through her again as the fiery liquid revived her body.

'I've relived the experience every day of my life since I lost the baby,' she said slowly.

'But it would have been so much easier for you if you'd shared it with me, Alyssa.'

She turned towards him. 'I couldn't do that, Pierre. You would have tried to persuade me that the fact I can't have children doesn't matter to you…just like you're doing now. But I know that sooner or later you would have regretted being married to me. You want a family so much.'

'We could have adopted a baby.'

Alyssa leaned back against the cushions and closed her eyes. 'Do you remember that conversation we had eight years ago, when you said you wanted your own flesh and blood as family?'

Pierre was silent for a few moments. 'Yes, I remember saying that.'

'You were speaking from your own experience, weren't you? Because you yourself were adopted?'

He nodded slowly. 'Yes, that's why I feel like I do. Because I was an adopted child myself.'

'But you were born on the island of Ste Cécile, where your father was the doctor, weren't you?'

'I was,' Pierre said quietly.

He looked down into the golden liquid he was swirling around in his glass. Alyssa could hear the rasping sound of his laboured breath. She should tell him she didn't want to hear the details and spare him what seemed to be an ordeal.

'Pierre, if you don't want to tell me any more, I—'

'I want you to know everything about me,' he said quickly, turning his face towards hers. 'It's important you know exactly why I've always had this longing for my very own family.'

She remained silent as she looked up into his eyes, feeling deep compassion for the emotions he was experiencing.

'My birth mother was a young girl who ran away from home with her boyfriend. I was told that they camped out on the beach until my adoptive father noticing that my birth mother was pregnant, suggested they move into our house where he and Sabine, my adoptive mother, could take care of them. Sabine couldn't have children, and she was over the moon when a baby was born in our house.'

Alyssa reached across and took hold of Pierre's hand. Her heart ached for him as she felt the tremors of emotion that were running through him.

'My birth parents readily agreed to the idea that I should be adopted by Claude and Sabine. So as soon as Claude's lawyer had dealt with the legal side of the adoption the young couple—who were only seventeen—left the island. Claude told me my real father was an impoverished student and my mother came from a prominent family who didn't want the news about their scandalous daughter to reach the press. That's all I was told.'

'But didn't you want to know more?'

'I was told that the young couple…my real parents…just wanted to get on with their lives and didn't want anything more to do with the baby…with me.'

'That must have been hard for you to accept,' Alyssa said softly.

Pierre's eyes flickered. 'I was twelve when my father…when Claude told me I was adopted. I prided myself on being a tough guy so I didn't let it upset me. And as for finding out that my real parents didn't want me…' Pierre shrugged. 'I can understand what they did. They were only seventeen, with all their lives in front of them. And it was the answer to a prayer for Sabine. She was the one who begged to be allowed to adopt me. Sabine had miscarried several times and she was desperate to have a child. Claude told me they regarded me as a gift from heaven.'

'At least you must have always felt wanted.'

'Oh, yes, I couldn't have wished for more attentive parents. But after I knew that Claude and Sabine weren't my real parents I felt different, somehow. And so I've never wanted to put another human being through what I went through after I discovered the truth. That's why I never even contemplated adopting a child when we talked about having a family.'

'I can understand why you feel like that,' Alyssa breathed, moving closer to Pierre.

'But that was then, Alyssa. Being with you again has proved to me that none of this matters any more. The only thing that matters is that we should be together…for the rest of our lives.'

He looked deep into her eyes. 'Alyssa, will you marry me?'

'Pierre, I can't! Sooner or later you would resent the fact that I can't give you the family you want.'

'No, I wouldn't. You're the most important part of my

life. For the joy of having you as my wife I would happily give up everything else. Now that you've told me why you broke off our relationship before, now that I know you're still the same Alyssa I knew, not some carefree, fun-seeking, shallow and unrecognisable woman, I'm not going to see you go away again. Please, Alyssa, say you'll marry me and—'

'Pierre, I want to marry you. But I know it wouldn't be fair. However you protest to the contrary, I know how passionately you feel about a family of your own, and I can't destroy your dream.'

Pierre leapt to his feet and began pacing the room. 'Alyssa, if you won't commit yourself now, would you consider seeing a gynaecologist and having an examination? If, as could happen, something can be done about your conception problem, would you then be willing to marry me?'

She stared across the room at him. He was standing by the window. They hadn't drawn the curtains and his tall, athletic body was framed by a background of stars and the glow of Parisian lights illuminating the night sky. At this moment she loved him more than she'd ever done. She wanted so much to believe that her childlessness wouldn't affect him, but she was convinced that it would eventually kill his love for her.

'I don't want to sound pessimistic, but if I couldn't conceive in two years…'

'Think positive, Alyssa. At least give it a try.' He crossed the room with easy strides, his eyes pleading as he bent over her. 'It doesn't matter to me whether you can give me a family or not. How can I convince you that you're all I want in life? If I can't convince you, then promise me you'll go and see a gynaecologist.'

'I'll think about it,' she whispered, almost to herself. 'Yes, yes—I'll get myself checked out.'

She heard Pierre's sigh of relief. His lips were hovering close to hers. She leaned forward and sought comfort in the balm of his kiss. Here—here was where she belonged. If only she could blot out all other considerations she would stay with Pierre for ever. As his kiss deepened she tried to immerse herself in the feeling of belonging, pushing away all the sensible considerations about how long Pierre would want her if she couldn't give him his much-wanted family.

Once bitten, twice shy, was the phrase that sprang into her mind. She closed her eyes as she remembered the distress she'd felt when Mike had rejected her because she couldn't give him a child, in favour of his pregnant girlfriend. She'd never loved Mike as she loved Pierre, but still, it had been hard to take. Rejection from Pierre would be impossible to bear.

He was holding her oh, so close now, his caresses soothing away her distressing thoughts. She moulded herself against his body, trying to fit herself into every muscular contour so that she would become one with the only man she'd ever really loved.

She sighed as he lifted her in his arms and carried her through to the bedroom. As he laid her down on the bed she allowed herself to drift off into a blissful state of mind where only the present had any meaning. The past was over, the future none of her concern. Only tonight mattered. They would live in their perfect world for a few hours…

Pierre's hand was on her shoulder, gently shaking her back to reality. She looked up and smiled the dreamy smile of someone whose body was utterly slaked with the passionate consummation of a night of lovemaking.

'I've brought you coffee,' Pierre said, sitting down on the edge of the bed.

He was wearing a black towelling robe and she could smell the aroma of his soap and aftershave. She must have slept on while he was splashing around in the adjoining bathroom.

'You haven't changed your mind, have you, Alyssa?'

She leaned back against the pillows as she reached for the coffee cup.

'About what?' she asked, playing for time as she tried to get her brain back from the realms of deep, love-saturated sleep.

'Will you definitely go to see a gynaecologist?'

She took a sip of her coffee. 'Yes, I'll go, but—'

'No buts!' Pierre said firmly, reaching forward to kiss the tip of her nose. 'And then, when you've seen the gynaecologist, will you reconsider my proposal of marriage?'

'I've already thought that one through. Pierre, let me see the gynaecologist and then…yes, I'll reconsider.'

'If you found yourself pregnant, would you marry me?'

'Of course I would! Finding myself pregnant would be a dream come true. But…' She stared at Pierre. 'Just because I've agreed to see a gynaecologist doesn't mean that a miracle will happen. I've still got the same scarred body, the same lack of function in…'

'Shh, you'll only upset yourself. Last night was the first time I didn't use a condom. Now that I know the problem, now that I believe there's a chance your surgical scars might have healed, I'm going to do my best to make you pregnant,' Pierre said, reaching across to remove the coffee cup from her hands. 'And there's no time like the present…'

Alyssa gave him a languid smile. Her body was still tingling from the aftereffects of their lovemaking. As she'd wakened this morning she'd thought she was totally satiated, but now, as Pierre's warm breath fanned her face, she felt the excited stirrings of liquid desire deep in the depths of her body…

Later that morning, Pierre and Alyssa hurried into the foyer of the *clinique*. It seemed natural to her that Pierre should still be holding her hand, but she couldn't help noticing the surprised but discreet glances from the medical staff.

They agreed to meet back at the apartment when they came off duty that evening. Pierre had insisted he would make the necessary arrangements for Alyssa's gynaecological examination. He was going to contact an eminent consultant in another hospital to make an appointment, and he was also determined to come with her.

'Gynaecologists usually prefer to meet the patient's partner, don't they?' he'd argued earlier this morning as she'd emerged from the shower to step into the large fluffy towel he was holding out for her. 'It makes sense to get the full picture. After all, it takes two to make a baby,' he'd added gently.

His caressing arms, encircling the towel with her inside it, had completely thrown her ability to think logically.

'Yes, they do,' she'd admitted. 'But announcing that we're a couple is a big step. It's tantamount to saying that…'

'It's saying that we're committed to each other,' he'd told her quietly.

Now, as she looked around the crowded foyer, she felt that everything was happening too fast. She was being manipulated. Strings were being pulled. She didn't feel in command of her future any more. After eight years of coming to terms with the fact that a family was a futile dream for herself, she now found she had to accept a whole new set of rules.

She'd steeled herself to accept what her gynaecologist had told her after he'd removed her Fallopian tube, along with the precious non-viable embryo, and after Mike's rejection she'd painfully accepted that she couldn't have a baby. But now…

She looked up at Pierre as he released her hand. For an instant she felt a sense of panic. What was she letting herself in for? Why had she come back and stirred up this hornets' nest which could only bring her more pain and suffering?

But as she saw the tenderness in his eyes she knew that her love for Pierre was the driving force that had brought her back to this situation. She had to go forward, for Pierre's sake. She couldn't disappoint him by refusing to be examined when he had such high hopes. Whatever the outcome, she owed him this.

'*A bientôt*, see you soon, *ma princesse*,' he whispered.

For a moment Alyssa thought Pierre was going to kiss her, but he merely turned and walked purposefully in the direction of his office.

She hurried away down the corridor, anxious to escape the questioning eyes. Standing in the lift, she pressed the button for the orthopaedics floor. She would go in and see her old patients and colleagues before she went back to obstetrics. At a time when you were feeling like a little-girl lost, you needed to see a few familiar friendly faces.

Alighting from the lift on the top floor, she reached for the nearest internal phone, calling obstetrics to let them know where she was. Jacqueline assured her that she wasn't required for another half-hour, when the consultant would do his round of the patients.

'Marie Lefevre has been asking for you, but I've told her that you'll be in later,' Jacqueline added.

'How is she?' Alyssa said, anxious to hear whether her ectopic patient was more settled than when she'd left her yesterday after her operation.

'She's much better physically. Emotionally she's still a bit down, but that's only to be expected,' Jacqueline said briskly.

As she put down the phone Alyssa reflected that Jacqueline was a no-nonsense professional. She cared for her patients with an expertise acquired over many years of hard work. It was unlikely she ever allowed her patients' problems to affect her own life when she went off duty. Not like she herself had done yesterday evening.

And look what that had got her! A proposal of marriage that she couldn't possibly accept under the circumstances. Nothing had changed in her body. Nothing had changed in her resolve not to tie Pierre to a childless marriage.

She put on a professional, confident smile as she walked in through the swing doors of orthopaedics. Whatever happened today she was going to give the patients her full, undivided attention, and leave her problems until this evening.

Making her way towards Henri Fontaine's bed, she found herself rewarded by the look of happy surprise on his face.

'You've come back, Dr Alyssa! What's the matter? Don't you like all those screaming babies?'

'Just called in for a few minutes to see how everybody is getting along. Can't keep away from you, Henri,' Alyssa quipped.

'We all miss you, Alyssa,' Henri said. 'I was asking Dr

Pierre yesterday how you were getting on delivering babies, and he told me it was your first day of actually working in obstetrics so he didn't know. He was planning to take you out last night to find out.'

Henri gave Alyssa a suggestive wink and lowered his voice. 'How did it go? The evening, I mean. I always thought you two should have got it together by now. I remember thinking to myself the last time you were working here at the *clinique* that you two were made for each other. What happened? Why didn't you meet up again sooner?'

Alyssa glanced round the ward. Nobody was remotely interested in their conversation, and with the clattering of the trolleys and trays nobody could hear what they were saying.

'Life happened, that's all,' she said quietly, and sat down on the chair at the side of Henri's bed. 'Don't you sometimes find, Henri, that circumstances beyond your control make it impossible for you to have everything you thought you might have?'

Henri pulled a wry face. 'Well, of course I do. But you're going to make it happen this time, aren't you, I mean you and Pierre…?'

Henri's big, kind eyes staring at her were almost pleading.

'I don't know. It's very complicated, Henri. Look, we shouldn't be discussing me. I've come to find out how you're getting on. How's the leg?'

She stood up and moved round to examine the badly injured leg, with its one gentamycin bead peeping out of the extensive wound.

'The wound looks much healthier to me,' Henri said. 'Those gentamycin beads that Pierre put in are a good idea.

He told me that they give off antibiotics for about three or four weeks which helps to get rid of any lurking infection.'

Alyssa nodded. 'That's right. When they've done their job, we'll remove them.'

'Does that mean another operation?'

'It's a fairly simple process. We'll just give you a local anaesthetic around the wound before we take them out.'

'Will Pierre do it?'

Alyssa smiled. 'I think he might, if you ask him nicely. It will depend on his schedule, of course, but why don't you check with him?'

'I'll do that,' Henri said. 'Trouble is, now that he's so important I don't like to keep on asking him favours.'

'Ask away, Henri,' Alyssa said, as she bent over the leg to examine the drainage tube. There was still quite a lot of fluid draining from the internal tissue of the leg.

'How long will it be before I'm up and about, Alyssa?'

She hesitated. She wasn't on the orthopaedic team any more, so it wasn't up to her to make a prognosis.

'You'd better ask your consultant, Henri,' she said carefully. 'It's going to take quite a while before everything is healed enough for you to start bearing weight on that leg.'

Henri nodded. 'That's what I thought. I'm resigned to it now. Can't hurry things. At the end of the day, for all the high tech equipment and knowledge you medics have, it's Mother Nature who's in charge, isn't it?'

'Very true, Henri,' Alyssa said, thinking how much this applied to her own precarious situation.

Sylvie was hurrying down the ward towards Henri's bed. 'Good to see you again, Alyssa. Would you like a coffee?'

Alyssa glanced at her watch. 'Just a quick one. Got to get back to obstetrics.'

'How are you getting on down there?' Sylvie asked, pushing open the door of her office.

Alyssa sank into one of the shabby but comfy armchairs. 'It's early days for me. I've only worked one day. I love delivering babies, but hate the trauma when things go wrong.'

'I thought you were looking a bit peaky when you walked out of the *clinique* last night. I was standing in the foyer and you looked straight through me as you went outside.'

Alyssa took a sip of her coffee. 'Did I? I'm sorry. I didn't see you, Sylvie.'

'I expect you were also in a hurry to go out on your date with Pierre,' Sylvie added with a huge smile.

Alyssa gave a start. 'How did you know about that?'

'It's the talk of the *clinique*! One of my nurses saw the pair of you walking along the path by the Seine last night, so deep in conversation that you nearly pushed her and her boyfriend into the river. And then our orthopaedic registrar just told me that he saw you both at a concert in the Ste Chappelle.'

Alyssa put down her cup. 'We both enjoy Bach's music. It was a very good concert.'

'And you were holding hands,' Sylvie finished, as if she hadn't been interrupted. Suddenly she laughed and clapped her hands together in delight. 'I am so pleased for you both! Pierre is a wonderful man and a great friend. I do hope—'

Sylvie broke off as someone tapped on the door. Alyssa stared up at Pierre as he stood in the doorway.

'Didn't expect to find you here, Alyssa,' he said in a bland, professional tone.

'Can't keep away,' Sylvie said, smiling at Pierre. 'If you ask me, I think she prefers orthopaedics to obstetrics.'

Alyssa stood up. 'I'm just on my way there. There's a ward round in five minutes. Thanks for the coffee, Sylvie.'

The sleeve of her jacket touched Pierre as she brushed past him. He looked down and smiled. 'I'm coming along to obstetrics later this morning. I have to write up a report on Marie Lefevre, our ectopic pregnancy patient, and I haven't got enough information in the notes I've been given.'

Alyssa nodded. 'I'll be there.'

She moved away quickly, desperately aware that Sylvie was scrutinising her as she stood so close to Pierre. Soon the whole of the *clinique* would be speculating on their relationship. They would be in the spotlight, and Alyssa wasn't looking forward to fielding questions about what was happening between Pierre and herself when the situation was still so unsure.

The ward round had been a useful way for Alyssa to get to know the patients. Frederic Massenet, the obstetrics and gynaecology consultant, was a patient, experienced, mature man who explained the patients' symptoms, diagnosis and treatment as his medical team followed him around the ward. Alyssa found that she was gaining a lot of knowledge about each patient, but one of the difficult aspects of obstetrics and gynaecology was that the turnover of patients was rapid. It was rare for patients to be in the ward for more than a few days, so she didn't get to know them as well as she would have liked.

But with Marie Lefevre it was different. She felt she had known this patient for a long time already. So many aspects of her situation were similar to her own, and she felt a deep empathy running between them. As soon as the ward round was finished she made a beeline for Marie's bed.

'How are you really feeling, today, Marie?' she asked gently. 'You seemed to be putting on a brave face during the ward round.'

Marie wearily raised her dark sad eyes.

'Well, you were there, Doctor. You heard the consultant telling me that the remaining Fallopian tube is scarred and may not be of any use when I try to get pregnant again. In effect he was saying he thinks it's useless, even though he used a lot of high-falutin medical jargon and tried to wrap it all up a bit. So how do you think I feel? Charles and I had set our heart on a big family. It just isn't fair.'

Alyssa was aware that someone was pushing through the curtains that she'd pulled as the tears started falling down Marie's cheeks.

'No, it isn't fair, Marie,' Pierre said sympathetically as he moved forward to sit on the bed so that he could take hold of the patient's hand. 'But it's happened before, to other patients, and eventually they've come to accept it.'

Standing there, looking at the tender scene which was too close to home, Alyssa could feel a lump in her throat that wouldn't move. Pierre was such a caring doctor. He would make a very caring father… She wished she could look into the future and see how this was all going to turn out.

'I don't think we will ever accept that we can't have children,' Marie said in a barely audible voice. 'We talked about having a family even before we got married, and—'

She broke off, unable to continue.

'I've come to help you, Marie,' Pierre said gently.

Alyssa sat down on the other side of the bed and wiped Marie's wet cheeks with a tissue as she listened to what Pierre was saying.

'We're in touch with a counselling service. I'm going to explain your situation to an experienced counsellor, who will then visit you here in hospital and help you to cope with the immediate future. Later on, when you feel stronger, you'll be able to see her again, and she'll explain the various options that are open to you when you decide to try and start a family again.'

'You mean fertility treatment, adoption and all that, Doctor?'

Pierre nodded. 'But those options will be a last resort. The body has a remarkable way of healing itself, given time. If you're patient, you may find that you can conceive naturally. Dr Massenet hasn't ruled that out entirely.'

Marie looked up, her face brightening. 'That would be wonderful. But I don't think it's going to happen somehow.'

'Yes, it's best not to be too optimistic at this stage,' Alyssa said quietly. 'You'll have to be very patient.'

Pierre looked across the bed at Alyssa, the expression in his eyes tender and sympathetic. 'I know we shouldn't raise our hopes too high, but there's no harm in being optimistic, is there? If there is a chance of natural pregnancy then it's more likely to happen to a happy patient than someone who's given up on the idea.'

Alyssa swallowed hard, knowing that he was referring to their own situation as well as their patient's. She turned away to reach for another tissue, this time for herself.

Pierre was writing something in the case file on his lap. 'Now, if you'd like to tell me about yourself, I'll take a few details and get in touch with our counselling service. That's if you'd like me to do that, Marie. It's up to you.'

Their patient hesitated before turning towards Alyssa. 'I'd prefer to give *you* my details, Doctor.' She turned back to look at Pierre with an apologetic expression on her face. 'Nothing personal, but I'd find it easier to talk to a woman doctor than a man.'

Pierre smiled and patted his patient's hand. 'Of course you would.' He looked enquiringly at Alyssa. 'Have you got time?'

Alyssa smiled. 'I'll make time for a patient as important as Marie.'

'Could you have your report on my desk by lunchtime?'

'I'm sure I could.'

Alyssa let Marie ramble on in an unstructured way, occasionally prompting her patient to get her back on course, and wrote down the details relevant to her case. Marie's overwhelming desire for a family was the most obvious factor in the case. Alyssa hoped that the counsellor would be able to give Marie some positive help in coming to terms with the uncertain situation.

As she closed the file and stood up Alyssa couldn't help wondering how she would have felt if she'd been offered counselling. She would have clutched at any straws back in those dark and desperate days, but would it have given her the courage to contact Pierre and enlighten him about her situation? It was purely academic now, so there was no point in speculating.

Drawing back the curtains from around Marie's bed, Alyssa smiled down at her patient. 'I'll come back later to see you, Marie.'

Marie's eyes pleaded with her. 'Thank you so much, Doctor. I feel you understand. It's almost as if you've been through this yourself.'

Alyssa remained silent, forcing herself to continue smiling. It wouldn't help the patient if she broke down and sobbed in sympathy. She had to remain professional if she was going to be a good doctor and help her patient get through the dark days ahead.

CHAPTER SEVEN

ALYSSA tapped lightly on the door of Pierre's office.

He stood up, going round the desk and coming towards her as she went in.

'I've brought the report on Marie you asked for,' she said, taking care to maintain her professional mode because she was unsure whether Pierre's secretary was still in her small room adjoining his office.

'Thanks, Alyssa.' Pierre said, taking the file from her.

He closed the door and, turning towards her, took her in his arms.

Feeling distinctly ill at ease beside Pierre's office door, knowing that at any moment they could be disturbed, she tried to release herself from his arms. But he was holding her too closely.

'Pierre! Don't you think someone might just walk in here?'

'Does it matter?'

She looked up at him. 'I don't know. I'm not the one in charge of the *clinique*.'

Pierre gazed down at her with a confident smile. 'Well, if that's your only concern, then...'

He bent his head and kissed her gently on the lips. Releasing Alyssa, he held both her hands in his while he stepped back to take a more careful look at her.

'I especially asked you to call in at lunchtime. As you know, everything stops for lunch in France, so I hope you'll have lunch with me.'

'I'd love to, but I haven't got much time. Spending half the morning with Marie has put my working schedule out.'

Pierre smiled. 'That's the English side of you talking! The English don't know the importance of relaxing in the middle of the day and having a good lunch. Lunch is essential to life in France, and especially in Paris. With the exception of medical emergencies, work can wait. As director of this *clinique*, I'm committed to looking after the health and welfare of my medical staff.'

She smiled up at Pierre. His boyish enthusiasm was infectious. 'Well, I could spare half an hour, perhaps, but…'

'Half an hour isn't long enough for a proper lunch!' Pierre said in a scandalised voice as he raised his hands in disapproval. '*Mon dieu!* We would barely have time to reach that small café in the Avenue Mozart, and I'm planning to take you along to a little restaurant near the Champs-Elysées where…'

'Pierre, perhaps we could go there this evening. I really do have to…'

'OK,' Pierre said grudgingly. 'We'll go along to the dining room. That won't take too long.'

'The dining room?'

Alyssa took a step backwards as she thought of the implications of being seen lunching with the *médecin-chef*. After her first day, when she'd had breakfast in the medical staff room, she'd been scrupulously careful not to be seen in any social situation with Pierre at the *clinique*.

'Yes, the dining room,' Pierre said, his eyes twinkling with amusement. 'Amazingly, that's where they serve lunch in this establishment. If we were in England we would have to go out and find a crowded pub, balance ourselves on a precarious bar stool and gulp down a curled-up cheese sandwich so that we didn't waste any time over our so-called lunch. Then we would spend all afternoon suffering from indigestion and working in a highly inefficient way.'

Alyssa gave a mock groan. 'You're incorrigible when you go all French with me. Don't forget I'm half-French, you know.'

He took hold of her arm and led her towards the door. 'Well, come and have a French lunch, then.'

The *clinique* dining room was crowded. All eyes seemed to be on her as Alyssa followed Pierre to a corner table that was still empty. It was at the far end of the room and she was aware that the noise of conversation had dropped dramatically.

She slid into one of the padded seats that flanked the walls.

'*Soupe, madame le docteur?*'

Alyssa, recognising the voice, smiled as she looked up at the black-and-white-uniformed waitress. Christine, who'd been here for years, not only served coffee and croissants in the medical staff room each morning, but also helped with lunch in the dining room.

'*Oui, s'il vous plait, Christine.*'

'*Et monsieur le médecin-chef?*'

Pierre smiled up the waitress. 'Do we have to be so formal, Christine? Couldn't you call me Pierre, like you used to before I was promoted to these great heights?'

Christine giggled. 'Not if I want to keep my job, *monsieur.*' She twinkled as she placed a bowl of spinach soup in front of Pierre. 'It's good to see the two of you together again. I was beginning to think you'd fallen out with each other since the last time you were both here.'

Alyssa looked across the table at Pierre as soon as Christine had left them alone again. 'Everybody in the *clinique* seems to be speculating about our relationship.'

Pierre gave her a grin. '*Eh bien*, what's wrong with that?'

Alyssa picked up her soup spoon, keeping her eyes deliberately on her plate. 'Well, I thought we should be a bit cautious while the situation is so delicate.'

'That's why I wanted to see you this lunchtime,' Pierre said softly. 'I've been in touch with Pascal Coumau, the gynaecologist I'd like you to see. He really is one of the top gynaecologists in Paris and he's agreed to see you next week. I'll make sure your work is covered by the obstetrics team for the entire day so that you can relax and take it easy afterwards.'

'Thanks, Pierre.' Alyssa put down her soup spoon. She'd eaten half the soup, but suddenly she didn't seem to have any more appetite.

'You're worried, aren't you?'

'Well, of course I'm worried... Sorry—I didn't mean to sound so fierce but it's bringing it all back to me and...'

Pierre reached across the table and took her hand in his. 'That's why we've got to get this problem solved once and for all. The uncertainty of not knowing can wear you down.'

Alyssa stared across the table at Pierre, grateful for his concern but sensing in her heart of hearts that it was most unlikely that her scarred body would have repaired itself so miraculously. She'd lived with the idea of sterility for eight years, and suddenly to have her hopes raised and probably dashed again fairly quickly would be heartrending. She couldn't help remembering how careful her gynaecologist had been to suggest that she should resign herself to most probably being childless.

As a doctor she knew that the body could sometimes heal itself, against all the odds, but she'd long since stopped believing in miracles.

Alyssa managed to swallow some of her main course. The *pommes frites* were delicious and the *pintade*—roast guinea fowl—was done to perfection. But she couldn't banish the worries at the back of her mind. Now that Pierre was involved it was ten times harder for her. If the examination proved her to be permanently sterile there would be two people plunged into despair.

Her mobile phone was ringing. She reached into her bag. It was Sister Jacqueline on the obstetrics ward. Across the table, Pierre was watching her enquiringly.

'No problem,' she told Jacqueline in answer to her short message. 'I'll come now.'

Switching off the phone, she stood up. 'Sorry, Pierre. An emergency situation on the obstetrics ward. Two patients in the final stages of labour and not enough staff on the ward.'

He stood up. 'I'll come with you. I should have been told there was a staffing problem.'

'Jacqueline says it's only just arisen,' Alyssa told him as they hurried out of the dining room. 'Two of the obstetrics medical team became ill and went home during the morning suffering from *la grippe*. Jacqueline thought the midwives could handle the workload, but now admits they need help.'

'I'll work with you, Alyssa,' Pierre said, as he pushed open the swing door that led into obstetrics.

'Delivery suite—*vite, vite!*' Jacqueline called as soon as they stepped inside the ward. 'Pierre, I was going to contact you to report that—'

'That's OK, Jacqueline. I understand the situation and I'm here to help. Don't worry,' he added as he saw the surprised look on the sister's face. 'I've had obstetrics training and a great deal of experience during my career. I've lost count of how many babies I've delivered—and not always in super-technical surroundings like we have here at the *clinique*.'

Alyssa and Pierre hurried down the ward, followed swiftly by a junior nurse carrying sterile gowns and masks for them to put on as soon as possible. After scrubbing up at the sink in the ante-room adjoining the delivery room, they hurried to take their places at either side of the delivery table in the first room.

Neither of them spoke as they prepared themselves. They were simply professional colleagues, all other personal considerations didn't exist for the moment.

'There's a problem here,' Catherine, the midwife, told them quietly. 'Labour has been prolonged—much longer than we expected.'

'Is the baby showing signs of distress?' Alyssa asked quickly.

The midwife nodded. 'Within the last few minutes there were signs that the baby is suffering, so—'

'Pierre!' Jacqueline appeared in the doorway of the delivery room. 'I need help in the next room. My patient is haemorrhaging.'

'I'll come now,' Pierre said, glancing across the table at Alyssa. 'You can handle this patient, can't you?'

'Of course,' Alyssa said, although she felt a moment of panic as Pierre disappeared into the next room. She'd delivered many babies herself, with varying complications, but Pierre's presence in the room had been very comforting.

Alyssa leaned over her patient, checking the monitor to find out for herself just how distressed the baby was. She glanced at Gabrielle, the young mother-to-be, and noted the signs of exhaustion showing.

'I can't hold out much longer, Doctor,' Gabrielle said.

'I can feel the baby pressing down on me and… Ooh, can I push now…?'

'Breathe into the Entonox mask,' Alyssa said, placing it over her patient's face. 'Hold off pushing, please, till I've checked that your baby is in the right position for delivery. Sister, take over from me here, please.'

As the midwife took over at the Entonox machine Alyssa quickly bent down to examine the birth canal. At the top of the canal the neck of the womb was fully dilated, but instead of the head presenting itself Alyssa could see part of a small buttock.

'It's a malpresentation,' Alyssa said. 'We've got to get this baby out now, Sister.'

Alyssa's mind was racing ahead as she thought of the options open to her. She could opt for a Caesarean section under general anaesthetic, or she could attempt to deliver the baby in breech position. Neither option was going to be easy at this late stage in the labour.

She decided to make one last attempt to deliver the baby down the birth canal before she had to resort to Caesarean section. She'd delivered several babies in breech position during her medical career. It was never easy, because each case was different, but she'd never lost a baby yet. And setting up a Caesarean section would involve calling in the anaesthetist, which would waste valuable time and cause more distress to the unborn baby and its mother.

Reaching her gloved hand up inside the birth canal, Alyssa felt her fingers make contact with the tiny buttock. She could tell that the baby was lying on its side; one tiny foot was already partially protruding through the neck of the womb. Grasping the foot gently but firmly, she eased most of the leg through the neck of the womb. The attached body was sliding with it; she could feel the buttocks coming along behind the leg and now the other leg, curled up against the small body, was being released.

Alyssa glanced up at her patient. The midwife was leaning over her, still holding the Entonox mask over Gabrielle's face.

'Gabrielle, can you give me one last push when you feel a contraction coming on?' she asked her patient gently. 'Your baby's nearly here; just one last effort from you and then…yes—yes…he's here. He's here…I've got him…'

Blood and mucus flowed out of the birth canal, but Alyssa was holding the slippery baby safely in her hands.

'*C'est un garçon*—it's a boy,' she told the young mother happily.

Carefully cutting the cord, she gave the tiny infant to its mother.

'He's wonderful!' the exhausted mother said, her buoyant spirits returning as she cradled her baby against her breast. 'I'm going to call him Thibault, after my father, who died earlier this year. He would have loved to see him but it wasn't to be.'

There was a movement at the door and the new father appeared. 'Sorry I had to go out, Gabrielle,' he said sheepishly. 'I would have fainted if I'd had to stay any longer.'

Gabrielle was smiling happily as she held her precious son.

'Fat lot of use you were, Gaston! You were supposed to give me moral support. But I'll forgive you if you promise to have the next one yourself.'

'Thank God that's not possible!' Gaston said, attempting to take hold of his newborn child and having great difficulty in holding the head in the right position. 'I think you're much better at this sort of thing than I am, Gabrielle.'

Alyssa was talking to the midwife about the postnatal

checks they were going to carry out on the baby and the mother when she heard the swing doors opening once more. Pierre walked into the delivery room.

'Everything OK here?'

'Mission accomplished,' Alyssa said, in a satisfied voice. 'A slight problem with a breech delivery, but the midwife and I coped.'

'Dr Alyssa was brilliant, sir,' the midwife said. 'I have to admit I was a bit worried. There was no time to lose if we were to save this baby.'

'And a lovely baby he is too,' Pierre said. 'May I hold him?' he asked the young father.

Gaston gave a beaming smile as he handed over the baby. 'What do you think of my son, Doctor?'

'I think he looks very healthy—and sounds it too!' Pierre was smiling as he handed over the lustily crying baby to the midwife so that she could start the postnatal checks. 'Doesn't sound to be anything wrong with this baby's lungs!'

'Thanks, all of you!' Gaston said, looking round the room at all the medical staff. 'I've brought a bottle of champagne so we can celebrate our baby's safe arrival. Have we got some glasses?'

Alyssa smiled as she watched the new father produce a bottle which had been smuggled in under cover of the voluminous green theatre gown he'd been made to wear. She'd never known this happen before in the hospitals she'd worked in—but then this was Paris, where life was always exciting.

The midwife produced some disposable paper cups from the ante-theatre, and Gaston did the honours.

'Well done, all of you!' Pierre said, raising his glass towards Alyssa. 'Here's to the doctor who brought little Thibault into the world. Santé, Alyssa!'

'*Santé*, Alyssa!'

Alyssa found herself blushing with embarrassment as the toast reverberated around the delivery room.

'I was only doing my job,' she murmured.

Jacqueline poked her head round the door. 'When you've finished in here, Dr Dupont, our patient would like to see you again. No hurry, of course. She's out of danger…'

'I'll be with you in a moment,' Pierre said, putting his plastic cup in the wastebin by the door.

Alyssa moved away from the table so that she could speak privately to Pierre. 'What was the problem with your patient?'

'Part of the placenta had been retained in the uterus after birth, so my patient had started to haemorrhage. Fortunately she'd been given an epidural anaesthetic so I was able to put my hand into her uterus and separate the placenta from the uterine wall. The bleeding is under control now and she's receiving blood intravenously.'

He lowered his voice. 'Don't forget to come to the apartment this evening, will you? We still haven't visited that restaurant on the Champs-Elysées I was telling you about.'

She smiled as she heard the shift in tone from professional to personal. Nobody in the room seemed remotely interested in their conversation.

'I'll certainly come to the apartment,' Alyssa murmured. 'But can we make a decision on the restaurant when—?'

'Dr Alyssa, would you come and look at baby Thibault?' Catherine called. 'Do you think he's showing signs of neonatal jaundice?'

'*A bientôt*—see you later,' Pierre said, disappearing into the next room.

Alyssa went over to look at the new baby. 'I noticed a slight tinge of yellow to the skin when the baby arrived,' she told the midwife. 'But it's not pronounced enough to need any treatment at this stage. I'd planned to take some blood so that we can ascertain the serum bilirubin level.'

'Is something wrong with my baby?' Gabrielle asked anxiously, raising herself from the pillows that had been placed behind her head and leaning over on her elbow to get a better look.

'It's just a slight discolouration of the skin, which is perfectly normal in some newborn babies, Gabrielle,' Alyssa told her patient quickly. 'We call it physiological jaundice and it's due to the normal breakdown of red cells. This occurs in all babies after birth, but in some of them the rate of breakdown is greater than the rate of elimination of bile pigments from the bloodstream. This accounts for the jaundice—the yellowing of the skin.'

Alyssa smiled sympathetically. 'There's absolutely nothing to worry about. It's only a tinge in the skin at the moment. If it becomes more pronounced later on we'll give baby Thibault some phototherapy.'

'What's that?' Gabrielle asked.

'We'll put him in a little cot with a blue spectrum of light above it. This will convert the fat-soluble bilirubin into water-soluble bilirubin, which can be excreted into his nappy. Meanwhile, I'd like you to drink plenty of water. You're planning to breastfeed, aren't you?'

Gabrielle nodded. 'Of course.'

'Well, we may step up the feeds if baby's jaundice becomes more pronounced, so you'll need plenty of milk.'

'What will happen if I haven't enough milk, Doctor?'

'We would give supplementary feeds with a bottle. But don't worry about that now, Gabrielle.'

'Thanks, Doctor. And thanks for explaining everything to me. It's good to know what's happening.'

Alyssa smiled and patted her patient's hand. 'You're both doing fine, Gabrielle.'

By the end of the afternoon the workload on the ward had eased considerably, and Alyssa found herself able to catch up on the routine work she'd intended to do that morning. The patients, who'd been waiting all day to see her, were very understanding when she explained the reasons for her delay in arriving at their bedsides.

It was dark outside when Alyssa hurried down the Rue de l'Assomption to Pierre's apartment.

Pierre thrust a glass of champagne into her hand as soon as she arrived.

Alyssa smiled up at him, clinking her glass against his. 'What's the celebration?'

'A continuation of the celebration we started in the delivery room. Only this time we don't have to drink from plastic cups…and this time,' he added carefully, 'it's looking ahead to a hopeful future for the two of us.'

Alyssa sipped the delicious champagne as she reflected that Pierre was taking their future together very much for granted. She was glad he hadn't said anything about babies, but she knew that was what was uppermost in his mind. She was certain that in his own mind Pierre was toasting the baby he hoped she would be able to have. It made her more and more nervous of the situation she'd found herself in.

'I haven't yet booked a table at the restaurant because I wasn't sure how soon you could get away,' Pierre said, placing both glasses on the coffee table in front of them as he drew Alyssa against him on the sofa.

'Would you mind if we stayed in tonight?' Alyssa kicked off her shoes as she leaned against Pierre. 'I'm feeling tired and it might be easier to talk here rather than in a crowded restaurant.'

'Of course I don't mind.' Pierre dropped a kiss on her head. 'What did you want to talk about?'

'Can't you guess?'

'Your gynae consultation?'

'Of course! What's he like, this consultant?'

'Pascal Coumau is kind, gentle and very thorough. We'll be in good hands.'

'We? I thought I was the one who was going to have the examination.'

'I'm in this with you all the way, Alyssa. If Pascal finds that there's no hope of a natural pregnancy then we'll go for fertility treatment.'

Alyssa stared at him. 'But I remember you saying that you wouldn't want to have to go through fertility treatment. I remember quite clearly. It was when we were sitting on that bench—our favourite bench—at the side of the Lac Supérieur in the Bois de Boulogne. We'd been discussing some new advances in fertility treatment that had appeared in a French medical magazine I'd borrowed from you. I'd only known you a couple of weeks, but you started to tell me about your dream of a big family and you said…'

Pierre's expression was troubled as he turned sad eyes towards her. 'Alyssa, that was eight years ago. That was what I believed in those far-off, carefree, idealistic days. But life changes and we change along with it.'

Alyssa reached out and took hold of Pierre's hand. 'I wouldn't want you to be tied to me if there was no possibility of a baby,' she said quietly. 'Pierre, you must see that if everything fails and—'

'Shh! Let's wait and see what happens, Alyssa.'

Pierre held her close to him, his lips seeking hers, and

as their bodies came together Alyssa felt the tug of desire rising again inside her. The physical act of making love with Pierre would soothe away her anxiety…

The sky was dark, with no sign of the moon this evening as Alyssa pushed back the curtains to look out over the rooftops of Paris. Through a gap in the tall buildings she could make out lights at the far side of the Seine. She turned her head to look at Pierre, still sleeping.

She reflected that there had been a certain poignancy about their lovemaking this evening. It was as if both of them had known that they were starting out on a great adventure. Alyssa would soon find out whether she could conceive naturally or whether she would have to embark on fertility treatment.

But what happened if everything failed? She stood up and crossed the room, easing herself back into the snug, warm bed, curling herself up against Pierre.

He stirred in his sleep and then opened his eyes. 'I dreamed you left me,' he said, still half asleep. 'But you've come back.' He pulled her closer against him. 'Alyssa, why don't you move into the apartment with me? After all, you did say you felt more at home here than anywhere else.'

Alyssa hesitated. 'That's true,' she said quietly.

Once again she felt that life was moving ahead too quickly for her. But she couldn't back out now she'd embarked on this adventure with Pierre. Still tingling from their ecstatic lovemaking, it was hard for her to make a decision. She had to put herself in Pierre's hands now and believe him when he said that she was more important to him than having a family.

He raised himself on one elbow, looking down at her with tender, expressive eyes. 'Was that a yes?'

'I think it was.'

'In that case you won't need to get up again tonight,' Pierre said sleepily as he drew her even closer into the circle of his strong, muscular arms.

'Or any other night,' Alyssa whispered, almost to herself.

But even as she snuggled against Pierre, feeling her strong desires blending with his, the doubts were still there. Her ultimate fear was rejection by Pierre when he regretted he was trapped in a childless relationship. She would never be able to forgive herself for changing her initial resolution—nor would she be able to bear the agony of rejection by him.

But—as she had to keep reminding herself—she couldn't back down now. And as Pierre's caressing hands coaxed her tingling body into a new sensual delirium she closed her eyes and gave herself up to the wonderful moment when their bodies would unite once more in ecstatic fulfilment…

CHAPTER EIGHT

ALYSSA looked along the street to the tall impressive building of the prestigious *clinique* that Pierre was pointing out to her and felt a moment of panic.

She'd insisted they take the Métro to the foot of the hill that led to the heart of Montmartre. Sitting in her seat close to Pierre as the carriage had rattled through the long, dark tunnels she'd felt as if time didn't exist any more. As long as she didn't reach journey's end she could still imagine that nothing was about to change between Pierre and herself.

But as they'd walked up the steep, cobblestoned road, with the impressive cathedral of the Sacré Coeur looking down on them, and as the minute hand on her watch had moved relentlessly nearer the time of her appointment, she'd been riddled with doubts.

Her eyes had been drawn to the shimmering silvery decorations festooned across the street for the festive season. Coloured lightbulbs adorned the façades of every building, and she'd tried desperately to forget her worries and absorb the spirit of Christmas. In spite of the cold, the doors of the little shops were open and blasts of enticingly welcome hot air had fanned her face as she'd walked past. She'd caught a glimpse of brightly coloured Christmas wrapping paper, cards, books and party clothes in the dazzlingly sparkling shop windows, but, however hard she'd tried, she hadn't been able to get rid of her apprehension.

Pierre, as if sensing her mood, had put his arm around her waist and drawn her towards a seat at the foot of the steps leading up to the Sacré Coeur. An artist who'd set up his easel close by, intent on capturing the beauty of the cathedral set in its well-tended gardens, had smiled at them as he paused between brushstrokes.

To Alyssa, he'd looked young, happy, and as carefree as she and Pierre had been in those far-off days when their love affair had been new and untried. She'd looked up at the clear blue sky, knowing that it was impossible to put the clock back. She had to go forward.

A wispy cloud crossed the sun, blotting out the feeble warmth. She shivered. Even though the sun was shining this morning, it had very little effect on the cold December day. A couple of days ago she'd had to buy herself a warm winter coat, and Pierre had pulled out a tailored black overcoat from the back of his wardrobe that morning. He'd asked her if she thought he would need it today and she'd advised him to wear it.

To all intents and purposes they were a real couple now. Living in the same apartment, eating together, sleeping together, making love together. In the week since they'd had lunch in the *clinique* dining room they seemed to have become accepted by the majority of the staff.

Alyssa hugged her own doubts about the situation to herself. She couldn't help realising that these doubts threatened the whole of her future with Pierre. But for the moment…

'You don't have to go through with this if you really don't want to,' Pierre said gently, drawing her hand into his, removing her new leather glove so that he could press her cold fingers to his lips. 'It's not too late for me to cancel the appointment.'

She turned to look at him, her heart so full of love for this wonderful man that she knew she would go through fire for him. But could she allow him to pledge his whole future to someone who might shatter his dreams?

She hesitated before her thoughts crystallised. 'I want to find out the truth.'

'So do I.'

Carefully he replaced her glove, raising his eyes to hers.

For a moment they remained close together, their eyes locked in a tender mutual understanding, before Pierre drew Alyssa along the ancient cobbled street towards the *clinique*.

'I'm relieved that we've come here,' Alyssa said as Pierre pressed the bell on the brass nameplate. 'Think of the rumours that would have flown around if I'd been examined at our own *clinique*.'

'That was one reason why I chose this place,' Pierre said. 'That and the fact that Pascal, besides being one of the best gynaecologists in Paris, is a friend of my father's.'

A look of concern crossed Alyssa's face. 'Your father?'

'My adoptive father—Claude.'

As the door was opened by a white-coated young man Alyssa felt uneasy about the fact that the eminent Pascal Coumau should be a family friend. She would have preferred to remain in a more detached, professional situation, where personal considerations didn't come into the equation, but it was too late now.

Once inside the *clinique*, Alyssa's first impression was one of quiet, calm, opulent surroundings, and subdued lights emphasising the sheen that appeared on the polished oak of the doors and wood panelling. Barely had they been asked to sit outside the great man's room before they were whisked inside by a dark-haired nursing sister in starched navy blue, with a shining silver buckle at her trim waistline.

'Pierre—good to see you again.'

Alyssa watched as Pascal Coumau, a tall, steely-grey haired man, probably in his mid-fifties but looking much younger, came forward from behind a huge mahogany desk, his hand outstretched towards Pierre. Briefly the men shook hands before the gynaecologist turned to look at Alyssa.

He gave her a genial smile which helped to put her at her ease. 'Welcome, Alyssa—may I call you Alyssa? Pierre has told me so much about you that I feel I know you already. Do sit down.'

Pascal returned to the other side of his impressive desk and wrote something on the case file in front of him. Alyssa had barely time to wonder what the consultant could possibly have deduced from their brief introduction before he began asking her questions.

An hour later Pascal was still questioning her. She looked sideways at Pierre, who was looking solemn. Her attention was beginning to flag, and she began to wonder whether all these questions about her previous medical history and her present general health were really necessary. Surely a physical examination would reveal more than she could possibly tell the gynaecologist.

As if reading Alyssa's thoughts, Pascal put down his pen and leaned back in his large leather chair. 'I think we all need a break. Would you like coffee?'

Pascal spoke into his intercom, instructing someone in the adjoining room to bring in a tray. 'Or tea, perhaps, Alyssa? Being half-English you might prefer...'

Alyssa smiled. *'Un café noir, s'il vous plaît, monsieur.'*

Now that the pressure was off her for the moment, Alyssa found she could relax. Sipping her coffee, leaning back against the plush, leather-buttoned armchair, she was able to look around at the tasteful surroundings. The book-lined walls, the antique pictures of old Paris all helped to take her mind off what might lie ahead of her.

'You're probably thinking I'm taking an extraordinary amount of details from you, Alyssa,' Pascal said at last, putting down his coffee cup on a small silver tablemat in the centre of his desk. 'But if you're to be my patient then I need all the background information I can get.'

'As a doctor, I can appreciate that,' Alyssa said, carefully placing her own cup on the silver tray at the front of the desk. 'But obviously I'm anxious to know what kind of physical examination or perhaps surgical operation you propose to perform on me.'

The gynaecologist placed both elbows on his desk and pressed the tips of his fingers together in a pyramid. He seemed to be considering Alyssa's question.

'Now that I've got the full picture of your background, Alyssa, we can proceed with the diagnostic and prognostic considerations. I'm relieved that both you and Pierre have been so frank with me.'

Pascal stood up and came round the desk. 'Firstly,' he said in a brisk tone, 'I'm going to perform an ultrasound scan on you to determine the extent of the injuries the ectopic pregnancy inflicted on your reproductive organs. Then I'll give you my findings and we'll take it from there.'

Pascal pressed a button at the side of his desk and the navy blue-uniformed sister came through from the adjoining room.

'If you'd like to follow Sister, Alyssa, I'll be with you in a few minutes.'

He turned back to look at Pierre. 'I think it would be a good idea if, initially, you stayed here, Pierre. I'll give you a thorough report at the end of the ultrasound scan. So if you'd like to make yourself comfortable...'

* * *

Lying on the ultrasound scanning table, looking up at the bright lights, Alyssa waited for Pascal to begin his examination.

'Was the coffee part of the pre-ultrasound treatment?' she asked the gynaecologist, nervously feeling a need to chat to him before the examination got under way. 'I've often had to remind patients not to empty their bladders before their ultrasound scan. Then I have to explain that ultrasound works best that way, and we get a better picture.'

The nursing sister, who was smearing ultrasound cream over Alyssa's abdomen, gave Alyssa a conspiratorial smile.

'As soon as Monsieur Coumau orders coffee for a patient I know I must get everything ready for an ultrasound scan,' she said.

Pascal smiled. 'Now, just relax, Alyssa. Have you got a good view of the screen?'

Alyssa assured the gynaecologist that she had an excellent view of the screen, which had been switched on above the end of the table.

'I'm just trying to orientate myself,' she said quietly, feeling her heart beating more rapidly as the picture of the various internal organs of her abdomen became clearer.

Pascal Coumau was moving the ultrasound scanner over her abdomen whilst keeping his eyes firmly on the screen. 'Here we've got the area where the left Fallopian tube was excised…looks like the ovary is missing as well… Yes— no ovary on the left side.'

'That's what I thought,' Alyssa said resignedly, closing her eyes for a moment as she remembered the first and last time she'd had an ultrasound scan. It had been six weeks after she'd lost the baby and the Fallopian tube in which it had tried to grow. The tissues around the affected area had been so badly scarred and damaged that it had been difficult to determine whether the ovary on that side had survived or not.

Apparently not. She opened her eyes and looked up at the screen again. 'What about the other side?' she asked. 'Can you move the…? Yes, leave it right there, please.'

She felt a pang of excitement as she saw her remaining Fallopian tube. From where she was lying she couldn't detect any abnormalities, but closer observation might reveal some flaws.

'The last time I saw this remaining Fallopian tube, soon after my operation, it looked completely unviable. The sides seemed to be attached to each other by adhesions. There was absolutely no way that an egg could travel down from the ovary. From the number of adhesions I saw eight years ago I couldn't understand why the surgeon hadn't excised this Fallopian tube as well as the one from where they took…they took the embryo.'

She drew in her breath to steady her nerves. She'd never dared to hope for a miracle, but this seemed the nearest thing. She looked up at Pascal.

'Would you like Pierre to come in and see this?' he asked gently. 'I didn't want him to be here if the injuries to your reproductive system were as bad as I first suspected. But I think you'll agree with me that—'

'You think there's a hope that I might conceive?'

Alyssa found she was holding her breath as she waited for the gynaecologist's answer.

'Let's get Pierre in first.'

It was mere seconds before Pierre arrived and took his place beside Alyssa. Taking her small hand in his, he looked up at the screen, narrowing his eyes as he focused on the picture.

'I'm no gynaecological expert, Pascal, but I would say—' Pierre broke off, his voice elated. 'That looks like a healthy Fallopian tube to me—and the ovary looks...' He glanced up at Pascal. 'Come on, you're the expert. What's your pronouncement on Alyssa's chances of conceiving?'

'Well, she's only firing on one ovary, and the egg has got to travel down this previously scarred Fallopian tube. But if all other conditions are right I think we might...'

'What other conditions are you talking about?' Alyssa asked quickly.

'Well, if I didn't already know, this is the point at which I would check on your social conditions,' Pascal told her. 'With patients whose background I'm not familiar with I would enquire if they were in a stable, settled relationship with a loving partner. That is one of the most important considerations. There must be no tension in the relationship.'

Pascal broke off and glanced at Pierre. 'Forgive me for mentioning this, but I gained the impression, from what Alyssa told me, that there was a great deal of tension in her previous marriage. This might have been an important factor in the reason why she couldn't conceive. The more settled and relaxed the situation between the prospective parents, the more chance we have of producing a baby.'

The gynaecologist gave them both a beaming smile. 'From the impression you've both been giving me, I presume you're planning a settled, permanent relationship?'

'Of course,' Pierre said quickly. 'I've asked Alyssa to marry me and...' He turned to look enquiringly at Alyssa, his tender eyes pleading for an answer. 'I know this is a strange place to ask you for the third time...'

'The third time?' Pascal's voice conveyed his amazement.

'Yes, the third time,' Pierre said. 'Eight years ago Alyssa asked me to wait until she'd finished her medical training. Then, only last week…'

'Excuse me while I leave you two lovebirds alone for a little while,' Pascal said, hurrying towards the door. 'I'll be back in a few minutes.'

Pierre leaned forward to kiss Alyssa's cheek with such tenderness that it brought tears to her eyes.

'I'm hoping I'm going to be third time lucky,' he told her huskily. 'Alyssa, will you marry me?'

'I will,' she said, softly.

Pierre drew her towards him, his kiss deepening as his lips claimed hers.

'I think you've just ruined your suit,' she said, as finally he pulled away. 'You've got ultrasound cream all over it.'

Pierre grinned. 'It doesn't matter. Nothing matters except that we're going to be together for ever.'

Pierre began planning their wedding as soon as they were in a taxi, heading down through the busy streets of Paris. The sky was darkening and the chill in the air had increased as they left the *clinique*.

'It looks as if it could snow,' Alyssa said, glancing out of the taxi window for a moment as she tried to rearrange her thoughts about the impending wedding.

When she'd awakened this morning, full of apprehension about her appointment with Pascal Coumau, she hadn't imagined that everything would happen quite so quickly.

'You're not taking this wedding seriously, Alyssa,' Pierre said, taking hold of her hand.

She turned back to look at him. 'Oh, but I am, believe me, Pierre. I'm just overwhelmed by the enormity of our new situation. I can't believe that I might be able to—'

She broke off, her eyes moist with tears. She didn't want to cry, here in the taxi, not when everything seemed to be working out for them.

Pierre drew her close and kissed her damp cheeks. 'Shall we leave the details of the wedding until later? You're understandably tired and—'

'No, let's talk about the wedding now—let's talk about it all the time,' she said, suddenly feeling happiness surge through her as she realised she could look into the future with hope again.

She and Pierre would be together for the rest of this year, for the whole of next year and for years, and years to come...

She put her hands on the sides of Pierre's face and drew his lips towards hers. 'I'm so happy,' she whispered, ignoring the fact that the taxi driver was watching them in his rearview mirror. 'Just now, when you suggested we get married before Christmas, I thought you were mad. I couldn't see how everything could be arranged in time. But now I can see that we don't need to worry about minor details.'

'Exactly! Leave the licence and all the paperwork to me, Alyssa. Just find yourself a beautiful wedding gown.'

'Couldn't we have a simple civil ceremony? Perhaps with a blessing in a church after Christmas, when we've got more time?'

Pierre hesitated. 'We've got to tell my parents yet. And when we do I have a feeling Sabine will want to be involved in the planning. She once told me she wanted me to be married in the church where she and Claude were married.'

'Where is this church?' Alyssa asked, a feeling of unreality sweeping over her.

'It's down in the south-west of France, on a craggy

promontory that overlooks the sea. My parents have retired to live in their holiday house down there. It's very beautiful—with a wonderful, rugged coastline—rather like our family home in the West Indies.'

'But would Sabine be able to organise a church wedding so quickly? It's less than two weeks to Christmas now.'

'Sabine is a very determined character. She will be able to get her own way with the clergy involved. She was born very near to the house she and my father now live in and knows lots of influential people in the area.'

Alyssa remained silent as a feeling of unreality swept over her once more.

'So, are you happy for me to give my parents the good news?' Pierre asked.

The taxi driver had pulled up in front of the apartment. Alyssa smiled up at Pierre.

'Of course. I look forward to meeting them. They must be quite a tough pair to have taken on someone like you from birth.'

'My father once said he hadn't much choice in the matter. Sabine gave him an ultimatum. Either he adopted me or she was leaving the island to go back to France.'

Pierre broke off to pay the driver, before putting his arm around Alyssa's waist and leading her up the stairs.

'Sabine sounds like my kind of woman,' Alyssa said with a wry smile as she waited for Pierre to unlock the door.

'You mean bossy?'

'Not at all! Strong, confident…'

'Same thing,' Pierre said as he swept her up into his arms and carried her over the threshold.

Alyssa laughed. 'What was that for? We're not married yet.'

Pierre pushed the door closed with his foot. 'No, but we soon will be.'

Carrying her through to the bedroom, he laid her down on the bed. 'I know you said you were tired earlier on, but…'

'I'm never too tired to make love with you, Pierre,' Alyssa whispered.

CHAPTER NINE

ARRIVING at the *clinique* next morning, Alyssa felt the world around her was totally unreal. It was less than two weeks to Christmas and it was an even shorter time to her wedding!

Pierre had gone in early because of a surgical emergency, so she'd had time to herself to think about everything she had to do. One of her first priorities must be to choose a dress. Perhaps she could fit that in this afternoon, if she could finish her scheduled work in time.

Stepping through the *porte à tambour*, she almost collided with one of the porters who was unloading a huge Christmas tree in the foyer.

The young man grinned. 'Sorry, Doctor! I've got to get this tree erected so you doctors and nurses can trim it this morning.'

'Come on, Alyssa,' Jacqueline said, as she hurried down the corridor into the foyer, followed by a couple of nurses from obstetrics. 'It's traditional that we all trim the Christmas tree, so I've left a skeleton staff on the ward while we work here for a few minutes. After that we'll trim our own tree up on the ward. The porters are bringing the boxes of decorations... Here they are... We always put the fairy on the top of the tree. That's when we need a tall man... Pierre!'

Pierre, arriving at the foyer desk, smiled as Jacqueline beckoned him over.

'I wondered how long it would be before I was needed,' he said, unwrapping the carefully cherished fairy. He looked down at Alyssa as he held the fairy in his hands. 'It's going to be a wonderful Christmas,' he whispered. 'Are you all right, Alyssa?'

She smiled. 'I'm fine.' She hesitated. 'A bit over-whelmed, but...'

'I'll help you all I can.'

'You can't help me choose a wedding dress,' Alyssa said firmly. 'I thought I could go round the shops this afternoon—unless I'm needed here.'

'I'll make sure you're not.'

Alyssa bent down to decorate one of the lower branches of the tree with silver stars. Pierre stooped so that he could whisper in her ear.

'I thought we ought to make an announcement about our wedding. How do you feel about that?'

Alyssa turned her face to look up at him and felt over-whelming love surging through her.

'Everyone will have to know soon, but will you make the announcement...perhaps when I'm out at the shops this afternoon...?'

Pierre leaned forward and squeezed her hand. 'Don't worry. They'll all be delighted with the news.'

More doctors and nurses were arriving in the foyer, un-packing the boxes of coloured glass balls, silver stars and tinsel. A porter hurried in with a trolley on which there were huge sacks of presents. These were to be stacked under the tree ready for Christmas Day, when they would be given to the children of a nearby residential home.

Jacqueline came round the tree to speak to Alyssa.

'I think we can be spared to go back to obstetrics now that half the staff seem to have arrived. We've still got our own tree to do. I've left a couple of nurses putting up coloured lampshades in the shape of stars. Come and see what you think, Alyssa.'

Alyssa looked at Pierre. 'I must go.'

Pierre looked down at her. 'Hope you find a beautiful dress this afternoon.'

Alyssa smiled up into his eyes. 'I feel as if I'm in a dream.'

Pierre bent down and whispered, 'So do I. A wonderful dream!'

As Alyssa started to walk away she noticed that Jacqueline was waiting for her at the end of the corridor. The knowing look on her face said it all. Nobody was going to be the least bit surprised when Pierre made his announcement this afternoon! But, unless there was an emergency, she would be shopping for her wedding dress when the grapevine began to buzz…

Alyssa's heart pounded with excitement as she went into the little boutique on the Rue de Passy. She'd often wandered past it on her way to the fruit market and she'd admired the elegant white dresses in the window. Now she was the one who had to choose.

A chic, immaculately coiffured elegant lady of a certain age came towards her.

'*Mademoiselle désire…?*' she enquired.

Alyssa swallowed hard. 'I'd like to look at wedding dresses.'

The lady smiled. '*Pour mademoiselle?*'

'Yes—yes, it's for me.'

'*Félicitations*—congratulations, *mademoiselle*! Come this way, *s'il vous plaît.*'

Alyssa was led into a large room at the back of the boutique, where several dresses were displayed on dummy models and many more were hanging on racks at the side of the room. Almost immediately her eyes fell on a chic white silk and lace creation which hung on one of the models. The tight bodice had puff sleeves and then fell in folds from the waist, fairly straight at the front but more generous at the back, so that it formed a small trailing train. The veil which crowned the outfit was of fine lace with a richly embroidered edge, not so opaque as to hide her face, but dense enough to create a little mystery, so that her face would only be revealed after she and Pierre were pronounced man and wife.

Her heart seemed to turn over at the thought, and she found herself shivering with excitement at what lay ahead of her.

'I'd like to try that one,' she said quickly.

A discussion on sizing followed, before the owner of the boutique helped Alyssa into the beautiful dress. It was—of course—too long for her, but she was assured that a seamstress would have no problem in making the creation fit her perfectly.

Alyssa stared at the stranger in the mirror. Was that really her? Was she really going to walk down the aisle of a church to where Pierre was waiting for her and…?

'I'll take it!'

'An excellent choice. *Mademoiselle* will make a perfect bride! One moment while I call my seamstress to check on the alterations, and then if you would care to return in three days' time the dress will be ready for you.'

Outside in the icy street, Alyssa felt as warm as toast. She positively glowed with happiness. The dress was the most expensive garment she'd ever bought, but she didn't mind dipping into the money her grandmother had left her. She felt sure she would have approved.

Her feet barely touched the ground as she hurried through the crowds of Christmas shoppers, glancing occasionally at the charmingly decorated shop windows. Her mind buzzed with the arrangements that she would have to make before she could be married.

Who could she possibly find to give her away in the church? It would have to be an old family friend. One of her mother's admirers who still lived here in Paris, perhaps? Yes, she knew the very one—and his phone number was in her address book.

The wedding was finally arranged for two days before Christmas. There had been a great deal of discussion between Alyssa, Pierre and his parents about whether it would be possible to have the wedding on Christmas Day, but in the midst of it all Pierre had stated quite clearly to his parents that he and Alyssa wanted to return to Paris on Christmas Eve.

They were both agreed that they wanted a quiet Christmas, on their own, in their own apartment, after all the excitement of the wedding and the organisation and plans leading up to it.

As Alyssa looked out of the window of Pierre's parents' house she reflected that she had been right in her assumption that his mother was a strong, confident character. As soon as Pierre had phoned to say that he and Alyssa were going to be married Sabine had wanted to take over all the organisation, right to the very last detail.

Initially Alyssa had been happy to go along with this. She had still been heavily involved with her work at the *clinique* and had had little time to spare. But on the question of which day they would marry neither she nor Pierre had given in to the parental idea that they should remain in the south-west until after Christmas.

Pierre had pointed out that he had to be back on the island of Ste Cécile early in the New Year, so would need time in Paris to organise his apartment and hand over his work at the *clinique* to Dr Cheveny.

Alyssa and Pierre had discussed the idea of spending Christmas in Paris with each other and decided that it *wasn't* selfish of them to want to be alone together, living in their apartment. After all, it would be their honeymoon.

From the moment Pierre had announced they were going to be married their time hadn't been their own. They'd both continued to work each day at the *clinique*, but had been overwhelmed by social invitations from the rest of the medical staff who all wanted to be a part of the happy couple's life.

They'd been invited to so many pre-Christmas parties that Alyssa had felt exhausted. They'd even hosted their own pre-wedding party in the Christmassy *clinique* dining room, which had been combined with a leaving party for Pierre now that Dr Cheveny was soon to return as *médecin-chef*.

They'd driven down from Paris the day before, and now they had a whole day in which to make final preparations. She wouldn't disturb Pierre, who was sleeping in a bedroom further down the landing. His final work schedule at the *clinique* had been excessive, and during their drive from Paris yesterday he had seemed very tired. As they'd driven off the ring road that skirted Bordeaux and headed out towards the coast Alyssa had insisted she take over the driving for the last few kilometres.

On arriving at the house Pierre had made an effort to be sociable with his parents, who had greeted both of them very warmly, but after a light supper they'd retired to their rooms. It seemed strange to be apart from Pierre in the night, but Alyssa had adhered to the sleeping arrangements which her hostess and soon to be mother-in-law had made for them. Sabine came from an older generation where the bride didn't sleep with the bridegroom until after they were married.

This evening they would go through a civil wedding ceremony in the nearby town of Arcachon, after which Pierre's parents were hosting a family dinner, but until then their time was their own.

Alyssa continued to gaze out at the beautiful view, wondering if she dared to slip out of the house and run down to the sea without waking anybody. The sea was angrily pounding on the shore at the end of the garden, the white-capped waves spreading their foam over the rocky beach. She turned to reach for the warm sweater she'd tossed on to a chair the night before.

The door was opening.

Pierre, wearing an old, unfamiliar brown robe, obviously borrowed from his father, came into her room, crossing the thick-carpeted floor in bare feet.

'I've missed you,' he whispered, taking her in his arms.

Alyssa sighed as she snuggled against the all familiar body of the man she loved so much. 'I've missed you too.'

Pierre looked longingly towards Alyssa's bed. 'Why don't we…?'

Alyssa adopted a mock scandalised expression. 'I'm saving myself for tomorrow night—my honeymoon night.'

Pierre groaned. 'In that case, let's go for a walk to burn off my frustration. I'll go and get dressed.'

Pierre unlatched the little garden gate that led immediately on to the shore and they ran hand in hand towards the pounding waves. Alyssa screamed with excitement as a huge wave bore down on them and they had to retreat to the safety of the upper tide mark, with its piles of seaweed and driftwood.

'The tide's going out,' Pierre said, drawing Alyssa close

against his side. 'I remember being brought here as a child for a brief holiday sometimes. It's been my parents' holiday home since they were married. Before that it belonged to Sabine's uncle, who left it to them in his will. They always made a point of coming back to France once a year, if my father could get away from his work in the West Indies.'

'Sounds idyllic!' Alyssa said. 'Living most of the year in the sun and then coming over to France for a holiday.'

'That's what I'm intending *we'll* do, Alyssa,' Pierre told her, as he kissed the tip of her nose in a playful gesture. 'You're cold. Let's go back into the warm house.'

'Not yet. I don't mind the cold. And I want you all to myself for a while. Let's walk; that will keep us warm.'

They walked briskly along the shoreline, talking excitedly like children making plans for a great adventure—except the adventure was their future together. As they ran a mock race back to the house Alyssa felt an overwhelming sense of belonging, of being exactly where she wanted to be, with the man who was exactly right for her.

The town hall was lit up brightly, as if to proclaim its importance at this festive season, declaring the pride that the citizens should feel for their town council. The imposing façade was festooned with chains of lights leading up to a huge star of Bethlehem at the apex of the collonaded front. Alyssa, following Pierre in through the covered portico, noticed a rough wooden shade which housed a nativity scene with the three kings bearing gifts for the infant in the cradle.

Reaching the main hall where the civil ceremony was to take place, she felt her heart lifting at the sight of the Christmas stars adorning the walls. Yes, Christmas was almost upon them, and here she was, at last going through the first part of her wedding ceremony. Tomorrow in the church would be even more daunting.

The room was crowded with people. Nervously smoothing down the skirt of her newly purchased, expensive Parisian suit, Alyssa looked around her. She hadn't a clue who most of these people were. She was grateful when Sabine, resplendent in a heavy silk dress with matching coat and a tiny hat perched on the top of her highlighted grey hair, introduced some of them to her, but the names didn't stick in Alyssa's mind. Seemingly most of the people were relatives or distant cousins of Claude and Sabine, who lived in the area or had travelled down from Paris.

A large, important, official-looking man called for silence and the conversation died down. Alyssa felt she was in a dream as she made the required responses in French. She glanced sideways at Pierre, who looked so handsome in a new grey suit. His responses were loud and clear. Alyssa had no idea what hers sounded like. The only important thing was that she made those vows…and meant to keep them. She prayed with her whole heart that Pierre felt the same way.

As they were pronounced man and wife Pierre turned to her. His kiss was brief, but oh, so sensual, giving a hint, a promise, of what was to come when all the ceremony had been dispensed with.

The waiting for the civil ceremony to begin had seemed endless, but now it was all over and Alyssa was caught up in a crowd of friendly, excited people, all wanting to kiss the bride, shake hands with the groom and congratulate them both.

Pierre succeeded at last in helping Alyssa into the be-ribboned car that was waiting outside for them. The driver began to sound his horn as soon as they drove away from the kerb.

'French tradition after a wedding,' Pierre said, in explanation of the honking of the horn which continued as they drove down the road that skirted the Bay of Arcachon.

Alyssa smiled. 'I know. I used to hear the sound of wedding cars when I was trying to sleep at my grandmother's as a child.'

'And to think we've got to do it all again tomorrow,' Pierre said, as Alyssa snuggled against him now that they had left the town behind them and were climbing the steep coastal path.

'I'm looking forward to our wedding in church,' Alyssa said quietly. 'The civil ceremony was only a formality, but tomorrow…'

'Formality or not, we're married, Madame Dupont,' Pierre said huskily, kissing her with a tenderness that took her breath away.

'I'm half-French you know,' Alyssa said, eventually forcing herself to move out of the circle of his arms. 'So I do know that tradition dictates we don't sleep together until after the church ceremony.'

Pierre groaned again. 'That's the second time today you've put me in my place. But I'm warning you, the honeymoon will be something out of this world.'

Alyssa leaned up to kiss his cheek. 'I certainly hope so.'

The car was coming to a halt outside Pierre's parents' house. Alyssa ran a hand through her hair, trying to restore it to the style which the visiting hairdresser had imposed upon it that afternoon.

'Leave your hair as it is,' Pierre said, ruffling her short blonde strands even more. 'I prefer you with the casual look. This is how I always used to remember you during the eight years we were apart.'

For an instant Alyssa could feel tears pricking behind her eyes. All those years she'd wasted without being close to Pierre. But now she could make up for it. Now she could begin to be a wife to him…and maybe…just maybe…the mother to his children.

The house seemed strangely quiet as they walked into the entrance hall, but then Pierre's mother came hurrying out of the salon to greet them. She had taken off her silk coat but remained in the tailored dress, which showed off her slim figure to perfection. Sabine was a handsome, well-preserved woman, and Alyssa could only guess at her age…late sixties, perhaps? Pierre's white-haired father was well into his seventies, and suffered with arthritis that forced him to walk painfully with a stick. But Sabine was still sprightly and full of boundless energy.

'We're in the salon, having an aperitif. Our dinner to-night is for close family only, so there will be just five of us.'

Alyssa looked at Pierre, who appeared as puzzled as she did. Five? Who was the other person who qualified as close family?

As Alyssa went into the sitting room she looked around at the Christmas decorations. Strands of silver paper were looped across the room and the Christmas tree, taking pride of place in the large window area looking out over the sea, was heavy with presents and coloured decorations of every shape and size.

A log fire blazed in the hearth. It was like any family gathering at Christmas…except who was the unknown man standing beside the Christmas tree? Alyssa remembered seeing him at the back of the crowded room in the town hall. No one had introduced her then, so she'd assumed he was one of the distant, obscure cousins.

He was a tall, distinguished-looking man, probably in his early fifties, his dark hair flecked with grey. He stepped forward now and came towards them, holding out his hand towards Pierre.

Pierre automatically put out his hand to the stranger.

'I'm very nervous about meeting you,' the man said quietly, still holding on to Pierre's hand. 'I'm André Filou…your father.'

Alyssa, watching Pierre's reaction, saw the blood drain from his face.

'You're…you're my father?' Pierre said, in a hoarse voice that was barely audible.

Alyssa swallowed hard. The moment was too poignant to bear. She held her breath as she waited for Pierre's reaction. He had every right to be upset with the father who'd abandoned him when he was a baby, but she knew that bitterness wasn't a part of Pierre's character.

Pierre reached towards his father. With a sigh of relief, André Filou put his arms around his son and held him in a firm bear hug for several moments.

The sound of a champagne cork popping brought Alyssa back to earth. The whole scenario had seemed unreal, but now Claude was holding out the bottle he'd just uncorked and the foaming champagne was spilling on to the carpet.

'One of you youngsters come and do the honours,' he called out from his chair. 'We've all got a lot to celebrate tonight.'

Pierre poured champagne for everyone and then, holding up his glass, he gave the first toast. 'To my beautiful bride.'

Alyssa smiled round and, raising her own glass, proposed a toast to her wonderful bridegroom.

'And I'd like to propose a toast to André,' Claude said, sitting bolt upright in his chair and holding his glass high in the air. 'It took some courage for him to come here and meet his son. To André!'

Curiosity was eating away at Alyssa. She longed to know all the answers. Why had it taken André so long to make contact? And why had he finally made the effort?

It transpired that André was a consultant surgeon at a hospital in Poitiers. He was married to a gynaecologist and they had two children, a boy and a girl, both studying medicine in Paris. The similarities in their lifestyles seemed endless, but Alyssa was still avid to know more about these newly acquired relatives.

During the course of the evening, whilst they were drinking their aperitifs and during the prolonged family supper, the story of what had really happened emerged.

André and Dianne had met when they were sixteen, on a skiing holiday in the Alps where different schools were amalgamated in one skiing course. This was how André, from a relatively poor family, had met up with the well-heeled Dianne. According to André, it had been love at first sight for both of them, and they'd taken every opportunity to be together.

A couple of months after returning home to Poitier André had got a phone call from Dianne. She was pregnant and desperate to know what to do. Her father was a prominent politician and Dianne hadn't dared tell her parents. André, being young and idealistic, had felt it his duty to protect Dianne. He'd drawn out savings from his bank, sent a cheque to Dianne and then the pair of them had flown, independently, to meet up on the island of Ste Cécile, with very little idea of what they were going to do when they got there.

Pierre reached across the table and topped up his father's glass with red wine.

'Thanks, Pierre,' André said, raising the glass to his lips. 'You've all made me so welcome since I arrived here today. And you especially, Pierre. I'm glad you're not angry with me.'

'Why should I be angry?' Pierre said. 'I have wonderful parents who have looked after me all my life. Claude explained to me when I was old enough to be told I was adopted that my mother had been very young and unable to keep me. Later he told me that she belonged to a prominent English family who would have disapproved of her having a baby when she was unmarried.'

'An English family?' Alyssa queried.

André smiled across the table at her. 'Yes, Dianne's mother was English. That was part of the charm for me—her beautifully accented French. When she was angry with me she would shout in a mixture of French and English which I found fascinating, and then…' André gave a sigh. 'But you don't want to hear about our stormy romance.'

'I gather you were very much in love with Dianne?' Alyssa said quietly.

André nodded. 'Yes, I was. But it didn't last. It was a young and immature love that didn't survive. My money didn't last very long out there on Ste Cécile. I bought a small tent, which I pitched under the palm trees near the beach.'

'And that was the first time I saw you, André,' Claude said. 'You were sitting on the beach with your heavily pregnant girlfriend and I started to worry about the pair of you.'

'I remember you persuaded us to move into your house so that you could look after us. Dianne was nearing her time and she'd had no medical examinations. I was so glad when you took over her antenatal care.'

'As I recall,' put in Sabine, 'Dianne needed very little persuasion to move out of that tent into a comfortable bedroom in our house. She was in a huge panic and didn't know what to do.'

Pierre nodded slowly. 'I understand what the poor girl must have been going through. Was that when the idea of adoption arose?'

Sabine nodded. 'Dianne begged me to adopt you. She said then she'd know her baby would have a good home. I was desperate to have a child myself, but my gynaecologist had told me I couldn't have children and...'

'That was when I phoned my lawyer in Paris,' Claude said, taking over the story from Sabine, who was overcome with emotion at the poignant memories. 'He drew up the necessary papers, and after baby Pierre was born in our house the lawyer flew over to finalise the details.'

'But why have you made contact now, André?' Alyssa asked quietly.

André's face clouded. 'Dianne was killed in a riding accident a couple of months ago. I'd had no contact with her since...since we left Ste Cécile, but I read it in the papers.'

'So did I,' Claude said. 'I knew that it was Dianne who hadn't ever wanted to make contact, so when I knew Pierre and Alyssa were going to be married I thought it was a good time for a family reunion. I know how Pierre has always longed to have his own flesh and blood around him.'

'You've been the best father I could ever have wished for, Claude,' Pierre said, his voice husky with emotion. 'But now that I've met my real father I feel totally complete. Alyssa and I will look forward to having you and your family joining up with my own family.'

André smiled across the table. 'I look forward to that. Are you planning a big family?'

'We're hoping so,' Pierre said in a confident tone. 'But if it's not to be we shall be happy in other ways.'

Alyssa held her breath as yet another toast was proposed, this time to their unborn children.

She couldn't bear to disappoint Pierre now.

CHAPTER TEN

THE ancient church stood on the walls of a small medieval town which was set on a rocky promontory on the shores of the Gironde. Usually cars were not allowed inside the walls of the town, but today the stately wedding car drove through the ancient stone gateway and drew up in front of the church already decorated by the congregation in preparation for Christmas.

Silvery lights shone around the porch and up the aisle. Roses, carnations and ferns had been arranged around the old stone windows through which shone the last rays of the late-afternoon sun.

The church seemed to be packed with everybody who'd attended yesterday's civil ceremony alongside other guests and well-wishers. Alyssa was poignantly aware of the beautiful, haunting music as she walked down the aisle, but the people, craning their necks to get a better view of the bride in her fabulous white gown, were a blur through her heavy white lace veil.

As she peered through it Alyssa knew that if she kept her eyes on that tall, dark-suited man waiting for her at the altar, she would survive the seemingly interminable walk.

She was holding on to the arm of an old friend of her mother's, who'd driven down from Paris for the occasion.

When Alyssa had phoned Jean Beauvois in Paris he'd said he would be honoured to give Alyssa away on her wedding day, and had admitted to a secret unrequited love for her mother many years ago.

Alyssa had been deeply relieved that Jean had agreed as she hadn't seen him since she was a child. Most of her grandmother's friends and relatives had moved away from Paris or had died, and her mother had been an only child. There had been no contact with her father since he'd walked out on them and Alyssa had long since accepted that he didn't want to acknowledge his first marriage.

The music stopped and she stood beside Pierre, making her responses, listening to his. The church was hushed and silent apart from the occasional cries of a small child who was rapidly taken outside by his mother so that the service wouldn't be disrupted.

And then Pierre was lifting her veil, kissing her gently, leaving a promise of their wedding night hanging in the air as he took hold of her hand and led her through the crowded church out into the cold December sunlight.

The church bells were ringing out into the air, the sea-gulls gave their distinctive cries as they swooped down, and the swishing of the waves on the shore formed a continual background of natural sound. Pierre was squeezing her hand and she felt her heart would burst with happiness.

'We're married,' he whispered as they stood in front of the flashing lights of the photographers.

'Can't believe it,' Alyssa whispered back.

The guests were beginning to move away down the hill to the hotel where the reception was to be held. Not long before they could be alone now…

It was only later that night, when all the guests had departed from the hotel, that Pierre and Alyssa were finally able to be alone. Alyssa looked around the bridal suite and drew in her breath.

Gently Pierre stooped down and began to undo the tiny silk-covered buttons at the back of her silk gown.

She looked down at the marks along the hem of her gown and smiled up at him. 'Most of the men I danced with have managed to leave their footprints on my dress.'

Pierre laughed. 'Every man in the room wanted to dance with you. You must be exhausted, but may I have the last dance with my beautiful bride?'

Pierre pressed a switch beside the bed and the quiet strains of a slow waltz filled the bedroom. Alyssa stepped out of her dress, allowing it to fall to the ground like a silken waterfall as Pierre drew her into his arms for their final dance.

As the music stopped he carried her gently over to their honeymoon bed.

'Happy?' he whispered, as she snuggled against him.

'Mmm…what do you think…?'

The lights of Paris seemed even brighter than usual this evening. In addition to the normal street lights, chains of coloured bulbs ran along each side, while shops, hotels bars and cinemas, decorated with every conceivable kind of festoon and trimming, blazed with the spirit of Christmas.

'Well, it is Christmas Eve,' Alyssa said, as she looked out over the Seine.

They were sitting in a small café on the Left Bank. It was one of the restaurants they'd frequented during their first wild fling together, but this was their first time there during this second time around romance.

'I didn't want to bring you here before I knew you were really going to marry me,' Pierre said, putting his hand over hers.

They were sitting in their favourite corner table. Looking around the crowded room, Alyssa could see other romantic couples holding hands. The candles on the table and on the Christmas tree in the corner of the room flickered. The room was strung with Christmas lanterns and the windows adorned with sparkling decorations created to look like snow.

'We mustn't forget we've got to do the rounds at the *clinique* tomorrow,' Alyssa said.

Pierre smiled. 'I won't forget. Even though I might become a bit distracted by our own Christmas celebrations.'

They finished their meal and walked out to hear the sound of Christmas carols echoing down the narrow cobbled side street. Students from the nearby university were making the clear Christmas Eve air resound with their harmonies.

Pierre hailed a taxi, which swept them off to the foot of the Eiffel Tower.

'You've got to see Paris in all its glory on Christmas Eve,' Pierre told Alyssa as he led her up the narrow iron staircase, gripping her hand as they made it to the *deuxième étage*—the second floor.

Laughing at Pierre's enthusiasm and energy, Alyssa agreed that in spite of being breathless it had been worth the effort. The whole of Paris was laid out in front of them, the magnificent city sprawling out on either side of the stately Seine. And, yes, she had to agree that the lights of Paris were even more spectacular because it was Christmas Eve.

They were moving off again.

Alyssa put her hands on Pierre's shoulders as they descended the stairs to saunter across the bridge that took them back to the Right Bank.

'Not too tired?'

'No, I love being out in Paris on a night like this. Pierre, let's just walk—let's lose ourselves in the streets and soak up the atmosphere of Christmas Eve in Paris.'

How long they walked, hand in hand, Alyssa had no idea, but the atmosphere was so electric she didn't want to stop—the happy crowds of revellers, the music as the doors of bars and restaurants opened, the pavement cafés where people laughed and joked as they stamped their feet to keep warm…

And then they found themselves climbing upwards, taking the cobbled street that led past the *clinique* where Pascal Coumau had given Alyssa such hope for the future.

Neither of them spoke about the problem that was uppermost in their minds.

Alyssa's period had arrived that morning. When she'd told Pierre he'd said it didn't matter that she wasn't pregnant. They were together, that was all that mattered to him, and besides, he'd found his father—his own flesh and blood.

But she'd seen the wistful disappointment in his eyes before he'd put up his façade of indifference. Life was a compromise, she told herself now as they mounted the steps to the Sacré Coeur cathedral. She had everything she could possibly wish for now. Everything except…

She deliberately blotted out her disappointment as, hand in hand, they went into the great cathedral. At the far end the choir were singing a haunting Christmas anthem. Alyssa bought a candle and lit it. As the small light flickered she found herself making a plea to her favourite saint that her final wish might come true.

But if it didn't…

She glanced up at Pierre, who had been watching her.

He knew what she was wishing, but he didn't speak about it. They had each other and that was enough.

He led her through the maze of streets surrounding the cathedral, past the artists in the Place du Tertre, who were still painting portraits by the light of the overhead lamps, and took her into a small café-bar called the Butte des Vignes. A young man was playing an accordion—all the favourite tunes she remembered from her Parisian holidays staying with Grand-maman. She leaned back against the chair and sipped at the cognac which Pierre had prescribed to keep out the cold.

'Happy Christmas, Alyssa,' he said, his voice husky. 'Next Christmas we'll be in the sun. I hope you won't miss the cold?'

Alyssa shook her head. Wherever Pierre was she would be happy.

Christmas Day at the *clinique* was a festive occasion. In the beautifully decorated wards Père Noel, in the shape of the small, rotund Yves Grandet, was doing his rounds whilst uttering lots of 'ho, ho, hos' amid hilarious laughter from the patients.

Pierre and Alyssa stopped off in the orthopaedic ward to wish Henri a Happy Christmas. Sylvie told them that the infection in Henri's leg was finally under control and they were hoping to send him home for New Year.

'Congratulations on your wedding!' Sylvie said, as they all stood around Henri's bed.

'Thank you,' Alyssa said. 'And thank you for looking after me when I first arrived.'

'I recognised at once that you were the one for Pierre.' Sylvie nodded with a smile. 'You pretended you couldn't care less, but I sensed what was happening.'

'So did I,' Henri said. 'You didn't fool me. And I'll expect a slice of the christening cake!'

'Me too!' Sylvie said.

Pierre put his arm around Alyssa in a comforting gesture as he sensed her unease.

'We're in no hurry,' he said evenly.

Taking their leave, they went on to the obstetrics ward. Marie Lefevre had remained in the *clinique* for extensive tests and counselling following her ectopic pregnancy. She had seemed much brighter when Alyssa had spoken to her a few days before.

'Happy Christmas, Marie,' Alyssa said, smiling down at her patient.

'How was the wedding, Dr Alyssa?' she asked, sitting forward in the chair beside her bed to grasp Alyssa's hand.

'Out of this world,' Alyssa said. 'But we're both looking forward to having some time to ourselves.'

'You're going out to live and work in the West Indies soon, aren't you?' Jacqueline said, coming across the ward to see them.

She was holding the latest arrival on the obstetrics ward. 'Thought you might like to see our Christmas baby. Baby Beatrice was born at two minutes past midnight this morning.'

'She's beautiful,' Alyssa said, taking the tiny little blonde-haired infant in her arms. The dear little rosebud mouth puckered into the makings of a smile.

'I know that's supposed to be wind,' Pierre said gently, as he touched the little mouth with his finger. 'But I like to think that Beatrice is smiling at us.'

'It's obvious the pair of you love babies,' Jacqueline said. 'I expect you'll have a big family out there in the West Indies.'

'Could be,' Pierre said lightly. 'We're leaving Paris in ten days' time.'

'We're going to miss you both,' Jacqueline told them, stretching out her hands to take baby Beatrice from Alyssa.

'And we'll miss all our friends here, Jacqueline.'

Alyssa looked enquiringly at Pierre. The seemingly endless rounds of patients and staff were taking their toll on her strength. She longed for the peace and quiet of their apartment...

The small tree in the corner of their sitting room seemed very tiny compared with the huge trees which had adorned each ward at the *clinique*.

'It's big enough for the two of us,' Pierre said. 'And next year...well, maybe next year we'll get a huge one.'

'Yes, maybe next year,' Alyssa said, thankful that Pierre hadn't voiced his obvious thoughts.

Alyssa picked up their plates from the kitchen table and took them over to the sink. Having had endless wedding feasts and a huge Christmas lunch, they had made their supper a simple affair. Alyssa had requested her favourite light meal, so Pierre had cooked a soufflé omelette.

He came up behind her now, putting his arms around her waist and holding her against him. 'Shall we have an early night? Catch up on our sleep?'

Alyssa turned and looked up into his eyes, revelling in the tender expression that mirrored her own.

'Can't think of anything I'd like better.'

She knew the time for feasting and celebration was over. Their real life together was now beginning. She had no idea what the future had in store for her, but whatever it was she was sure that Pierre would always be at her side.

The last few days had cemented their love. Not only was Pierre her lover, her husband, but he was her best and most trusted friend. She couldn't ask for more than that.

Or could she...?

EPILOGUE

ALYSSA ran down the beach into the blue sparkling sea. It was a perfect morning. The sort of morning when she was used to settling herself amongst the rocks for an hour or so, before it was time to help Pierre with his morning clinic.

Out here on Ste Cécile she had more time for relaxing than she'd ever had in her life. For a couple of hours each morning she helped Pierre in the clinic adjoining their beautiful spacious house. After that, if there were patients to be seen on the surrounding islands, she would sometimes go in the boat with Pierre to lend a hand, or simply chat with her new-found friends.

She and Pierre made a point of having lunch together, either at the house or in one of the tiny restaurants here on Ste Cécile or on the surrounding islands. But usually by the middle of the afternoon they were free to spend time on the beach—swimming together, exploring the rocky creeks in their boat or simply lying under the palm trees, their fingers interlaced, as they talked endlessly about every subject under the sun.

Every subject except the one which was usually uppermost in their minds.

Pascal Coumau had told them to wait a year before they gave up the idea of having a baby naturally. He'd given Alyssa his personal phone number, telling her to call him any time she was worried. Only three weeks ago she'd been on the point of picking up the phone. One year on,

179

with Christmas almost upon them, there was no sign of their much-wanted baby.

But two weeks ago her period hadn't arrived. And she was always on time.

Slipping off her sandals, she remembered how she'd tried to contain her excitement. She hadn't dared to raise Pierre's hopes. For the first few months of their marriage she'd reported every little detail of her menstrual cycle to him, but lately she'd been more guarded.

There was no point in both of them breaking their hearts. They had a wonderful life here on the island—she couldn't wish for a more fantastic husband, their love grew stronger every day, and yet when a much-wanted child hadn't materialised…

'Hey, wait for me!'

She turned at the sound of Pierre's voice. He was running down the beach towards her, clad only in black swimming trunks. She held her breath at the sight of his firm muscular body. It was only a couple of hours since he'd held her in his arms and her body was still tingling from their lovemaking.

He flung wet salty arms around her. 'You do realise you've still got your dress on, don't you?' he said, laughing as the spray from the waves made them both even wetter.

'I didn't intend to swim,' she said, turning over on to her back, her cotton dress floating around her like petals on a large flower. 'I just got excited about something, and you were down in the clinic treating that patient who'd called in early, so…'

'Hey, steady on. What was so exciting that you forgot to take your dress off?'

His face in the water was oh, so close to hers as she continued to look up at the heavenly blue sky. A sky that

would never look the same again now that the miracle had
happened.

'I…I did a test…just now…and…'

'Tell me—tell me, Alyssa!' Pierre was holding her in
his arms now.

She trod water. 'We ought to swim back to the shore.
It would be such a pity if we both drowned now…now
that…now that we're going to be parents…'

Pierre drew Alyssa on to her back as if he were lifesav-
ing. 'Don't move another muscle, Alyssa. I'm holding you.
Now, just relax and—'

'Pierre, I'm not ill. I'm going to have a baby.'

'I know, and it's the most wonderful day of my life. I
love you so much Alyssa. I always did, but now…'

Calm and relaxed, now in dry clothes, Alyssa sat on the
terrace holding a glass of freshly squeezed orange juice in
her hand. Pierre had insisted she do nothing for the rest of
the day, having decided that her early-morning dip had
been too strenuous in light of her condition.

'You're not going to cosset me all through the nine
months, are you, Pierre?'

He smiled. 'Of course I am. We're not going to take
any chances with this one. I'll cosset you through your
first pregnancy, but after that, when you're an experienced
mum, we'll take it in our stride.'

'Don't you think we ought to start phoning people?'
Alyssa said. 'All those pointed remarks that Sabine has
been making to us. And what about André and his wife?
They're becoming as bad as Sabine whenever they phone.'

'We'll tell them all together when they come out here
for Christmas—our first real family Christmas together.'

'I'm so looking forward to Christmas this year.'

Pierre smiled lovingly. 'Make the most of it. It will

never be just the two of us again. Baby will make three. We'll be up to our eyes in nappies.'

'I don't mind if you don't,' Alyssa said softly, as she realised that, against all the odds, all her dreams had now—unbelievably—come true.

Pierre folded her in his arms. *'Ma petite princesse,'* he whispered. 'I love you so much. I've always loved you, since the first moment I saw you...but now...even more than I ever thought possible...'

Alyssa closed her eyes as she revelled in being oh, so close to Pierre. She would take such care of this precious baby inside her. She was strong and healthy now, but her experience of obstetrics had taught her never to take anything for granted in a pregnancy.

She gave a little shiver as a trace of doubt ran through her. Pierre held her away from him and his eyes searched hers.

'You're going to be fine! I just know that this time next year—'

Alyssa put her finger against his lips. 'Don't say it, Pierre,' she whispered, and she realised that he too, after all his medical experience had taught him, was having doubts.

EPILOGUE TWO

ALYSSA waved her hand as the hire car taking the last of the Christmas guests away disappeared down the drive. It had been a hectic Christmas and she was looking forward to having some time alone with Pierre and baby André. Looking at her son now, sleeping peacefully in Pierre's arms, she felt a surge of love for both of them.

'Let's have a drink on the terrace, Pierre, now it's just the three of us.'

Pierre smiled. 'I must admit I'm looking forward to having the pair of you to myself. Sabine can be so bossy where babies are concerned!'

Alyssa laughed. 'Sabine is an expert on everything! But she really enjoys herself spoiling André, doesn't she? And all those presents they brought!'

'And André is over the moon that his grandson is his namesake.'

Alyssa sighed contentedly as she gently took André from Pierre and sank down into one of the cane chairs on the veranda.

Pierre handed her a glass of champagne. 'It doesn't seem like three years since we married.'

Alyssa eased herself back against the cushions. 'In some ways it's flown past, but in others...'

She swallowed hard as she looked at Pierre.

He put out his hand and tilted her chin so that she was looking up at him. 'You were marvellous all the way through your pregnancy. You needn't have worried.'

'But I couldn't help worrying,' Alyssa said quietly.

Pierre nodded understandingly. 'Neither could I. But we needn't have worried, need we? And next time…'

'Next time?'

'I would say you're a natural at having babies, Madame Dupont.'

'Is that your considered opinion, Doctor?'

'Absolutely!'

'I'm glad about that, because it just so happens that I did a test this morning, and…'

'You're not going to tell me that—?'

Alyssa nodded and smiled.

'Alyssa—I think you're wonderful!'

'Well, you did give me some help. And I won't be scared of going through this pregnancy now that I know everything is OK. What shall we call this one? If it's a girl we could call her Sabine, and if…'

'Alyssa, let's leave all that for the moment and just think about ourselves,' Pierre said gently, taking their baby from Alyssa's arms. 'Come upstairs and we'll put André in his cot. We need some time alone together.'

'Don't worry. We'll always make time for each other,' Alyssa said softly as she walked up the stairs beside her husband and son.

And later, as she lay in Pierre's arms, listening to the sound of the waves on the shore, she knew that her dream, her wonderful dream, was going to get better as each year passed.

Modern Romance™
...seduction and
passion guaranteed

Tender Romance™
...love affairs that
last a lifetime

Sensual Romance™
...sassy, sexy and
seductive

Blaze™
...sultry days and
steamy nights

Medical Romance™
...medical drama on
the pulse

Historical Romance™
...rich, vivid and
passionate

27 new titles every month.

*With all kinds of Romance for
every kind of mood...*

MILLS & BOON®

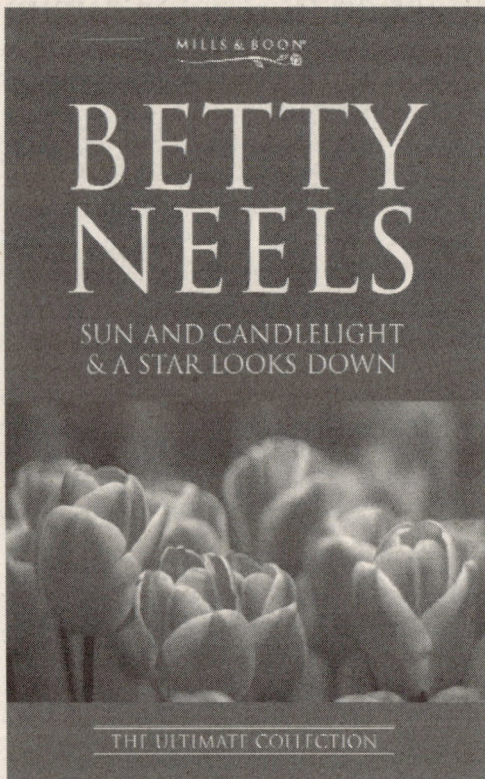

FREE

2 BOOKS
AND A SURPRISE GIFT!

We would like to take this opportunity to thank you for reading this Mills & Boon® book by offering you the chance to take TWO more specially selected titles from the Medical Romance™ series absolutely FREE! We're also making this offer to introduce you to the benefits of the Reader Service™ —

- ★ FREE home delivery
- ★ FREE monthly Newsletter
- ★ FREE gifts and competitions
- ★ Exclusive Reader Service discount
- ★ Books available before they're in the shops

Accepting these FREE books and gift places you under no obligation to buy; you may cancel at any time, even after receiving your free shipment. Simply complete your details below and return the entire page to the address below. *You don't even need a stamp!*

YES! Please send me 2 free Medical Romance books and a surprise gift. I understand that unless you hear from me, I will receive 4 superb new titles every month for just £2.55 each, postage and packing free. I am under no obligation to purchase any books and may cancel my subscription at any time. The free books and gift will be mine to keep in any case.

M2ZEC

Ms/Mrs/Miss/Mr ....Initials ....

BLOCK CAPITALS PLEASE

Surname ....

Address ....

....

....Postcode ....

Send this whole page to:
UK: FREEPOST CN81, Croydon, CR9 3WZ
EIRE: PO Box 4546, Kilcock, County Kildare (stamp required)